THE CASE OF THE
LONELY ACCOUNTANT

Also by Simon Mason

A Killing in November
The Broken Afternoon
Lost and Never Found

THE CASE OF THE LONELY ACCOUNTANT

Simon Mason

riverrun

First published in Great Britain in 2024 by

riverrun

An imprint of

Quercus Editions Limited
Carmelite House
50 Victoria Embankment
London EC4Y 0DZ

An Hachette UK company

A CIP catalogue record for this book is available
from the British Library

TPB ISBN 978 1 52942 599 4
EBOOK ISBN 978 1 52942 600 7

1

Typeset by CC Book Production

Printed and bound in Great Britain by Clays Ltd, Elcograf S.p.A.

Papers used by riverrun are from well-managed forests and other responsible sources.

For Eluned

On Thursday, 30 October 2008, Donald Bayliss, Chief Accounting Officer and Vice President for Asset Management (Europe) at Marshall Worth, went missing. He was based in the Marshall Worth office in Bournemouth, one of the banking giant's many global hubs, and early in the afternoon of that day, asking to be excused for a moment, he abruptly left the meeting he was chairing in the boardroom on the third floor and fifteen minutes later exited the building. The following morning a sports bag containing the suit and shoes he'd been wearing was found on a sea-facing ledge of the Haven Hotel at the mouth of Poole Harbour, where the tides are particularly strong.

Three witnesses claimed to have seen Don in and around Bournemouth that afternoon. At three thirty, an

1

acquaintance encountered him in a beachside café by the pier, sitting alone with a cup of coffee. When greeted, Don appeared confused, saying, 'Don't worry about me, *I'm* all right.' A little while later, according to a man in Parkstone, a suburb of Poole, Don visited his house asking to see a bicycle he was selling, but disappeared while the man was fetching it. Finally, that night, a fisherman at the mouth of the harbour reported seeing him sitting smoking a cigarette on the rocks directly below the ledge where Don's bag would be found.

Beyond these sightings and a certain amount of conjecture, the police investigation made no progress and, a year later, concluded that Bayliss had likely drowned himself, the result of intolerable pressure at work. It had been the very worst time of the financial crash. His body was never found, but in October 2015, in accordance with the seven-year-rule, he was legally presumed dead.

Eight years later they reopened the case and Dorset Police called me in to explain why.

I haven't always been a 'Finder'; events conspired to push me in that direction. I grew tired of institutional life within the police and when I was offered an attractive redundancy package I took it. Other, more personal, events deepened my interest in those people who may no longer be living but who occupy in our imaginations a tangible, sometimes unbearable, reality: I mean the missing, the lost, the regretted, the badly remembered or badly suppressed, the blamed and the desired, those whom time will never simplify. So I became a freelance specialist, hiring myself out to any police force that feels a need, as many do, to employ a third party rather than put strain on an already overstretched team or increase the payroll. Over the years, I've worked with many forces in many different parts of the country, trying to find those missing presences.

But I'd never worked before with Dorset Police. Arriving in Bournemouth by train, I took a taxi from the station to my hotel, asking the driver to take a detour alongside Meyrick Park in order to glimpse the offices where Don Bayliss had worked. I was disappointed, however: they were entirely hidden behind trees, low-rise buildings set among the golf course and sports ground of the park and guarded from casual public access by manned booths around the perimeter. On we went to the Ventry Arms in Branksome Park, a quiet suburb of large Edwardian villas and modern mansions, not quite Bournemouth, not quite Poole, but indeed, as the taxi driver informed me, laid out along a stream which was once the ancient boundary between the two towns, and also between the counties of Hampshire and Dorset, and the dioceses of Salisbury and Winchester. It was late May, a warm day, and the Ventry Arms, a pleasant villa of red brick, steep gables and bow windows, sat in sunlight on a graceful ellipsis of lawn trim and bright as a green on a golf course. There was a taste of salt in the soft air, a hint of the seaside, the promise of a mild climate. Its climate is famous. Here, a hundred and forty years earlier, the tubercular Robert Louis Stevenson came

4

for the sake of his health, living just a few streets away in a villa where he wrote *The Strange Case of Dr Jekyll and Mr Hyde*, a copy of which I had in my bag.

After unpacking, I went for a short walk, out of the inn, across the road and down an unnamed lane curving along the top edge of Branksome Dene Chine, one of several steep-sided, wooded gorges running south, at last emerging out of the thick greenery on to an open bluff, the beach below me and ahead of me the sea, a broad expanse of almost colourless blue wrinkling in the breeze. I stood there a moment, looking out. Then I turned and looked back across Branksome Park, where, hidden somewhere among the far trees, was the house where Don Bayliss had lived.

Before I visited the house, I took a taxi into Bournemouth, to meet my liaising officer, a detective sergeant called Louise. The district station is squashed into the centre of the city, concealed behind offices and blocks of student accommodation in a built-up but still developing area, where new roads have the tendency to revert suddenly to old roads and new roundabouts to lack purpose. Louise was based here, in a room with a view of a brick wall and background noise of drills and motors. I had not worked with her before.

She explained the situation. Don's widow, Mrs Bayliss

(she still called herself this although she had remarried), had contacted them to say that she'd found something 'odd' at home. She'd been sorting out things in her attic and, among the papers and files from her late husband's home office, she'd found a wallet containing business cards. There were many cards in it and she was nostalgically browsing through them, recognising some of the names and companies Don used to mention, Bud Forster at Lehmann, Richard Woolner at Citi and so on, when she came across a card which didn't seem to fit. It was a garish gold colour, cheaply produced, unlike the discreet, high-quality cards of the banks, and printed with nothing but a name – Dwight Fricker – and a contact number. Curious, she tried the number and found it was unobtainable. She googled the name and got a single hit: Dwight Fricker, convicted in 2015 of fraud, trafficking, prostitution, assault and extortion. At that point she rang the police. She was alarmed that her husband might somehow have got mixed up with this gangster and that it may have something to do with his disappearance.

Louise slid a photograph across the desk. It showed a balding, chubby-faced, middle-aged man with the mild, slightly myopic expression of a child's favourite uncle. This was Don Bayliss. According to Mrs Bayliss's original testimony, Louise said, his biggest vice was coconut mushrooms.

I asked what sort of involvement Mrs Bayliss thought her husband had had with Dwight Fricker, and Louise said Mrs Bayliss had no idea. Louise herself had no idea. It could be nothing at all, she said. In fact, she hoped it was.

Her phone rang and her face took on the damped-down expression of someone habitually overworked: she was due in a meeting. She had a small budget, she told me, pushing a folder across the desk, enough for about a fortnight's work. I pointed out that this was not likely to give me enough time to find Bayliss, if indeed he were still alive, which itself seemed unlikely, and she replied that the task in hand was not finding Bayliss, but checking out the Dwight Fricker link and explaining, to the satisfaction of his widow, how his card came to be in her husband's possession. That was all. Mrs Bayliss, she added, with a pause for emphasis, was a prominent town councillor and active on the local police board, a forceful lady of strong opinions, not above making public criticisms of the police. Keep that fact front and central, she said, and then with a hurried look at her watch she was gone, and I stood alone in her office, with the chubby face of Don Bayliss smiling up at me benignly from her desk.

The Bayliss house stood on the corner of Western Road and Mornish Road, deep in the most exclusive part of

Branksome Park, an enclave of small mansions of brick and stucco with tennis courts, swimming pools and orangeries lapped in the luxuriant greenery of mature woodland. There was the sound of birdsong, of water running somewhere, a fountain perhaps, and the motor noise of a ride-on lawn-mower. The house was called 'Sunrise' and it was so lavish that, even taking into account his doubtless large Marshall Worth salary of fifteen years earlier, it seemed not to fit with my idea of Don Bayliss, the diffident, homely man in the photograph. When I announced myself at the intercom, the tall crenellated gates swung slowly open and I walked between lines of dwarf palms up the drive to the front door, which opened as I approached, and Mrs Bayliss appeared, a graceful, smartly dressed woman with a beautiful head of hair dyed gold. I knew from the file that she was sixty-three years old, had been forty-seven when her husband disappeared, and had recently remarried. She shook my hand in the brisk, efficient manner of busy people, asked me to call her Sylvia, and led me along the hall into a large reception room with high-gloss stripped pine floorboards and white walls, furniture with hard, straight lines, stylish *objets d'art* and an altogether fashion-conscious decor. Above the wide fireplace was a marble mantelpiece on which were arranged a dozen or so thank you cards which, she said, had arrived from local residents expressing their gratitude for her recent success in closing down a housing development in the area. There were two giant sofas in dove grey, and I sat on the one that seated five, and Sylvia stylishly arranged herself opposite me on the one that seated seven. I admired the room and she blushed slightly and told me that, when Don hadn't been working in his study, he'd loved to sit in it, and I asked her if Don had been a connoisseur of art and she smiled. No, she said with another blush, that would be her. But Don had shared her tastes. He loved the garden too, she told me, and though he hadn't had the time or indeed the inclination to do the work, which was generally left to her and the gardener, he loved to sit out on the patio or in the gazebo and enjoy the peace. He had not been a very active man, she told me, with a smile that managed to be both wistful and a prompt to move the conversation on.

I did not at first ask her any questions about the card, however. I asked if she remembered how Don had been behaving in the weeks prior to his disappearance. Well prepared, she immediately repeated what she'd told the police in the original investigation. It had been the worst time of the financial crash, for months Don been overworked: he had to curtail his volunteering work, the Samaritans phone-line, for instance, which he did on Tuesday evenings. His back went into spasm, his usual weakness, and he had been seeing his regular Alexander Technique teacher in London.

His annual autumn bronchitis was very bad; she'd taken all his cigarettes off him and forbidden him to smoke. In short, he was in a state. Although Marshall Worth was weathering the financial storm better than most, it continued to be a desperately difficult time, and, frankly, she said, she'd never thought the company had done enough to support Don, who was left shouldering everything they could dump on him. He had an over-developed sense of responsibility. All this was very interesting. I asked her if she would be able to give me a list of Don's various routines during those few weeks – the Samaritans hotline, the Alexander Technique sessions and so on – and she made a note to do so. Then she again showed signs of wanting to move the conversation on, but before raising the subject of Dwight Fricker's card, I asked her if she agreed with the official finding that her husband had taken his own life. She was not afraid of the question but sat considering it for a moment. On the whole, she said, she believed it, yes. She itemised her reasons. Work pressure was obviously a factor: there had been a moment when it appeared that Marshall Worth might close down their UK operation entirely, and Don had felt very acutely the responsibility that senior managers like himself had for all the employees. She remembered too that, although Don had never mentioned suicidal thoughts, or indeed spoken explicitly in favour of suicide, he had always been a supporter of assisted dying, thinking it acceptable, civilised in fact, to take the decision to end one's life if the pain of living became too great. Finally, she said, Don was not a strong person, he lacked the stubborn sometimes unattractive willpower that other, less sympathetic people, draw on to get them through difficult times. He tended to give in. These points she delivered fluently, as if they had been formulated a long time ago, but now she hesitated. There was something else, she said, flushing, something more intimate, which had been in her mind recently. She remembered that for a few weeks before his disappearance Don's sleep had been disturbed: from his bedroom (they had slept in separate beds, a convenience given Don's frequent restlessness brought on by his back pain), she had heard him mumbling and occasionally calling out.

'He kept saying the word *sorry*.'

Of course, she didn't know what had been in his dreaming consciousness but it was possible, she thought, that he had been expressing regret for what he was about to do. Anyway, she went on now, to get to the point, the reason for reopening the case was the card, the card was the important thing. It had shaken some of her assumptions. At last, she took it from her bag and handed it to me. Louise's description had been accurate: it was a cheaply produced affair of the simplest possible design; as I held it between my fingers I could feel the soft, almost spongy quality of the paper. It had been such a shock finding it, she said, and she was bewildered by what it might mean. For the time being, I replied, that was my position too. She looked at me, I thought, with disappointment, but before we could continue that conversation I asked her if I might see Don's study. Now she gave me an impatient look. The study had long ago been cleared out, the only things from it that remained were stored in the attic, she didn't think there was anything there that would be of interest. But I persisted and she got up and led me back through the hall and up the staircase, which was decorated in the same manner as downstairs, with white walls, chic fittings and original art work. As we went, I complimented her on it all again and asked if she had chosen the things here too, and she said yes, throughout the whole house in fact. She'd always had a very clear idea of what she wanted, she said, even when very young, she was that sort of person.

'Don was the opposite,' she added, 'so we complemented each other.'

On the second floor we encountered a man who came suddenly out of a bedroom holding a tissue to his face in the manner of someone having a nosebleed, and Sylvia said, 'Not now, Desmond,' and we went past him and up a final flight of steps.

'My husband,' she commented.

We went at last into the attic, a huge, dim space running the whole length of the house, the rafters of the roof lost in shadows above us, our footsteps echoing on the wooden floorboards. Here and there were sofas and other articles of furniture covered in sheets, rolls of carpet, crates stacked neatly, one on top of another, and finally, at the far end, the contents of Don's home office – desk, chair, bookcases, piles of folders – which she'd kept for no particular reason and in fact had never looked at until she decided that the attic needed sorting out. I asked her how much time Don used to spend in his home office and she told me that in the fraught and busy months prior to his disappearance he'd hardly emerged from it.

She left me then and I browsed for a while among the boxes and shelves, going through desk drawers, occasionally examining something but generally just nosing around. I didn't hope that something might suddenly transform itself into a 'clue', I wasn't particularly looking for clues, indeed don't particularly believe in them, at least not as a distinct category, I wanted simply to develop a feel for Don Bayliss, to catch a hint of the man himself, if I could, in the things he had surrounded himself with. But I couldn't. Everything there, without exception, was nondescript, generic, bland. No flourishes, no quirkiness, no luxury, no tat, nothing worn or damaged, but nothing new, nothing personalised, only the ordinary, the standard, the anonymous. A complete, almost aggressive lack of self-expression, the opposite of the well-defined expressiveness of the rest of the house which so vividly reflected his wife's tastes. There was a hint of something more intimate, perhaps, in the old CD player with a disc of Erik Satie's *Gymnopédies* still in it, the trace of a personal mood in his choice of music, though the pieces are universally known and the strange melancholy they express has become a sort of general cliché. I turned to Don's bookcases. I'm a reader, always attracted to other people's bookshelves. Don's collection was small; most of the books were technical, financial or legal, and well-used. The rest, half read or even unopened, were generic airport reads, thrillers I could imagine him picking up on his frequent trips to the Marshall Worth offices in New York. I was about to turn away when I noticed that one book had fallen behind the others on the shelf, and I pulled it out. It was Virginia Woolf's *Mrs Dalloway*. Alongside the others, it seemed out of place, literary, a story not of adventure but of the consciousness. Unlike the other novels, it was well-thumbed, there were places marked in the margin with asterisks and, towards the end of the novel, a passage had been underlined.

There was nothing else of interest in Don's belongings

and I made my way out of the attic. As I passed among all the domestic lumber, my eye was momentarily caught by something different, a crate of baby things, a suddenly much more personal touch and a puzzling one because I knew Don and Sylvia had no children. Everything in the box was new, clothes and toys, some of them still unwrapped, but dusty now; and name tags had been sewed into the collars of two or three of the little suits: *Adrian Bayliss*. I went on again through the general accumulation of sofas and light-stands, rugs and picture frames, feeling the faint energy, common to attics, of discarded lives, jettisoned pasts and unrealised futures, and made my way downstairs, thinking of the very different sorts of life which a man might make or leave behind or, indeed, never experience.

Back in the living room, I asked Sylvia if Don had been a big reader of fiction and she smiled. No, she said. He read technical books, financial reports, he read the local newspaper from front to back every week, but she didn't think she'd ever seen him reading a novel. Not once, she said. I asked what Don's leisure interests had been, and she repeated that he worked hard at Marshall Worth, under-took a little voluntary work, and apart from that, tended to recharge his batteries by watching television or sitting out in the garden, not doing anything much, just recuperating. She said again how tired he had been in the months leading up to his disappearance, he was so busy fighting fires at the office, he really had no energy left when he came home, which was generally late, sometimes in the early hours of the morning. She repeated her criticism of Marshall Worth. Don's biggest problem, she went on, was his good nature, his habitual self-deprecation; he found it impossible to say no to other people's requests and ended up doing twice as much work as anyone else. He didn't have the strength to resist. He didn't like arguments or disagreements, hated drawing attention to himself, and one aspect of this was that he wasn't always forthcoming or communicative in general, even about important things. He bottled things up, pretended to himself that they weren't as bad as they seemed. As an example of this, she told me that Don had been on the Tube train that had been destroyed in the 7/7 bombings in London but for several days hadn't even mentioned it to her. He'd been unharmed and didn't want to upset her, he'd said, didn't want to make a fuss. That's why Dwight Fricker's card had alarmed her. If Don had got himself into some sort of 'situation' involving this Fricker, he might not have known how to get himself out of it.

I thought of Don in the café on the afternoon of his disappearance saying, 'Don't worry about me, *I'm* all right,' exactly like someone not wanting to make a fuss.

But of course, she added, she couldn't imagine how Don

16

might have become involved with someone like Dwight Fricker, it seemed unbelievable.

I asked if Don had had any history of mental illness and again she took no offence at my question but considered it carefully. She was aware of the hypothesis, suggested in the original investigation, that he had suffered a sudden and catastrophic breakdown prompted by his overwork, causing him to lose a sense of what he was doing and even who he was, leading perhaps to his eventual suicide. But she had rejected this. Don had always been completely sane, she said. He was perhaps the most level-headed person she had ever known. And, in any case, she didn't think a breakdown could account for any possible involvement with a gangster. Temperamentally, Don was completely conformist, timid, passive, fearful of infringing conventions, even inadvertently, let alone of breaking the law.

I asked then if she thought Don was a man who kept things hidden from her. Now, for a moment, she appeared uncertain. She would never have thought that, she said carefully. Never. They knew each other inside out. Perhaps, she said after a moment, her discovery of Dwight Fricker's card had temporarily disturbed that belief, but she trusted that there would be an explanation, a simple explanation, she fancied, and that I would soon find it. I told her that I had arranged a visit to Dwight Fricker in Belmarsh Prison,

17

and she wished me good luck and said that she looked forward to hearing my report of it.

She came with me as far as the front door. By the way, she said, as we walked together, she was assuming that I hadn't found anything of interest in the attic. I didn't mention the copy of *Mrs Dalloway*, which, it seemed clear, she would not have known anything about, but I mentioned the box of children's things. At once, her demeanour altered. She looked away and momentarily fell quiet. I was beginning to apologise before she recovered. She'd forgotten they were up there, she said, still looking at the floor. When she was young and newly married, she'd wanted children, had tried to conceive, but it had proved difficult. She had various sorts of treatment, after a year or two became pregnant, but then, four months later, after undertaking the usual preparations for a child, including the purchase of various items, miscarried.

'It changed me,' she said.

After her miscarriage she decided there could be no children. Her experience had traumatised her.

I offered her my sympathy. Had Don been badly affected too, I asked? No, she replied. Don had never shown much interest in starting a family. In truth, he had been relieved that, after all, his life wasn't going to be disrupted by children, that he could pursue his career and keep to his routines without domestic distractions. As for herself, she went on, brisk again, there are plenty of ways for a woman to keep busy. She'd been involved in local politics now for nearly forty years. People recover after traumas. They adapt and go on and live the life that's possible for them, they absorb their sadness. 'They do things with their lives,' she said, again the busy councillor. 'Why should husbands be the only ones with careers?'

As we parted, she asked me if I had any more questions about Don.

'Only one,' I said. 'Did he wear a watch?'

She looked at me hard, suspecting me perhaps of frivolity.

'Of course.'

I thanked her and walked back down the driveway through the sumptuous gardens of the Bayliss house and out of the slowly swinging automatic gates.

Back at the Ventry Arms I read through the account of the original investigation which Louise had given me at the station. In the limited time available, they'd been thorough. As well as the usual local campaign, interviews with work colleagues, neighbours and so on, they'd liaised extensively with transport providers, the ports, coastguards and nearby airports, with Interpol and other agencies with contacts abroad. They'd worked particularly closely with the ferry services operating out of Poole Harbour en route to destinations in France. It was quite clear: there was no sign of Donald Bayliss leaving the country.

Before dinner, I had some time to kill and walked from the Ventry Arms through the quiet avenues of Branksome Park to the Alum Chine Road, where Robert Louis Stevenson's house once stood. The Luftwaffe destroyed it in the war and now it is merely a gap between houses, in which a memorial garden has been planted. Here, the artist Singer Sargent had come to paint him, conjuring up an emaciated figure pacing and smoking in the darkened rooms, here Henry James came to talk shop, and here Stevenson wrote both *Kidnapped* and *Jekyll and Hyde*. Nevertheless, he hated Bournemouth, living among its respectable matrons, he said, like 'a weevil in a biscuit'.

It was late afternoon and the light was failing but though the narrow garden was shadowed by overhanging trees, the foundations of the house were still dimly visible in the grass, impressions of cramped rooms, where Stevenson must have paced and smoked and talked and written. He was ill much of the time, an invalid confined to bed upstairs, scribbling in the dark as he choked. Beyond the foundations, at the far end of the garden, the ground suddenly falls away. It is the Alum Chine, a jungle of untamed rhododendron and lopsided pines hung with creepers, bushes and shrubs growing out of the crumbly slope descending steeply into thicker shadows; and I stood there for a while, thinking that Stevenson may well have stood on exactly the same spot, wrapped in a shawl perhaps, or sitting in a bath chair, gazing down into the darkness, dreaming his stories of violence.

And I wondered why a man, walking naked into the sea to kill himself, would keep his watch on. The bag of Don's clothes found on the ledge at the Haven Hotel contained everything he'd been wearing, down to his shoes, socks and underwear, and included his phone, wallet, handkerchief, pack of breath mints, signet ring and wedding ring. But no watch.

The dining room of the Ventry Arms was modest and pleasant, overlooking the spotlit lawn and the avenue beyond. I sat in the bay window and had the sole and a fruit salad, and read the opening chapter of *Jekyll and Hyde*, in which Utterson the lawyer first hears about Mr Hyde, a man known to no one but so repugnant he brings out a cold sweat in all who come across him. He has been seen violently trampling a child but, when accosted, coolly pays off the parents with a large cheque drawn on the name of the eminent scientist Henry Jekyll. A terrible complicity between the two is at once suspected – though the truth, as is well known, will be much stranger and much worse. Over my coffee, I thought again of Stevenson in his lair among the matrons dreaming up this tale of brutality lurking in the most respectable places, and I thought too of the way Utterson and his friend Enfield immediately agree never to talk about the issue again, or to ask any more questions about it, as if the most terrible thing of all is not the evil act itself but acknowledgement – and knowledge – of it; and finally I thought of that copy of *Mrs Dalloway* in the Baylisses' loft, with the underlined passage. It was about the character Septimus Warren Smith, a shell-shocked war veteran. The passage read: 'The young man had killed himself; but she did not pity him.' It was the bit about pity that had been underlined, not the bit about the suicide.

A voice spoke and I looked up. A woman stood there. I'd seen her before when I checked in, a woman in braids wearing a tracksuit. She had a beak-like nose and she bobbed it at my book.

'Folio Society edition?'

I acknowledged it. Her accent was Antipodean.

'Love that Mervyn Peake.'

Peake had done the illustrations for the 1948 edition.

'Love the way his Hyde looks exactly like Paddington Bear.'

It surprised me and made me laugh, and she laughed in turn. I asked her where she came from.

She told me New Zealand and perhaps she was going to say more but her phone rang and she nodded at my book again and smiled and moved away out of the dining room; a few moments later I caught a glimpse of her going up the stairs. I examined the Peake illustrations of the malevolent Edward Hyde. I hadn't noticed before but the dumpy figure in the shapeless overcoat could easily have been mistaken for the amiable bear.

Armed with my police credentials, I made my way past the security booth at the perimeter of Meyrick Park and into the MWFG building. At the start of the crash, the Marshall Worth Financial Group were the seventeenth largest international bank by market capitalisation, and although they were no longer that, they had survived the crisis and made a recovery. With Goldman Sachs, JP Morgan Chase and Barclays, they remained one of the biggest investment banks in the country. Their offices were, as I had imagined, smart in the corporate style, all muted tones and high-quality fittings. Framed slogans hung in Reception, unimpeachable sentiments of tolerance, diversity and innovation, there was an air of calm, a sense of orderliness, but as I sat there waiting to be escorted to my meeting I tried to imagine what it had been like in the October of 2008, when Don Bayliss had excused himself from his meeting upstairs, walked out of the building and disappeared. It had been a time of great tension, emotions running high. Marshall Worth had secured a bailout from the Fed earlier in the year but no one knew exactly how much damage had been done, how much bad debt was still hidden in the accounts. As the effects of the crash spread through the industry, banks went bust, employees lost their jobs, senior figures struggled to keep their companies afloat; by October, the collapse of the entire sector seemed possible. At the same time, public feeling was intensely hostile – there were no possible excuses the banks could offer for what they had done – and it was not yet clear that the politicians would save them. I imagined that a man who didn't like fuss or disagreements, a man burdened with an over-developed sense of responsibility towards others, would have found it difficult.

The young woman appointed as my minder arrived to take me through security and upstairs to the boardroom, where three older members of staff who remembered Don were waiting to talk to me. Two were from Don's old accounting team, one from HR, and they were sitting together at the end of a long shiny table. On the wall behind them was a large screen. One side of the room was panelled in the same shiny wood as the table, the other was ceiling-to-floor window with a view of the pleasant golf course below and, beyond, the office blocks of downtown Bournemouth. This was the view Don would have had as he stood there, chairing the meeting on his last afternoon.

Rachel and Felix, the two members of his accounting team who had been in that meeting, described it for me. It had begun at one thirty, about half an hour late. Twenty or so of the staff were there; Don, recently returned from New York, was briefing them on the company's ongoing attempts to identify and ring-fence toxic liabilities. It was a fairly technical briefing; as always, Don delivered it in a calm, methodical manner. He was standing at the far end of the table, putting up information on the screen, patiently explaining things, asking if there were any questions, moving on. Rachel remembered that his posture was awkward, that sometimes he put his hand at the base of his back, as if to ease some discomfort; she knew he'd been suffering from back pain, and she guessed that the plane trip had made it worse. Felix remembered that he looked tired. Jet lag, he assumed. Don was speaking quietly – but then, Felix said, he always spoke quietly.

I asked about the moment when he'd left.

It was about quarter past two. Don had already finished his presentation. He was sitting again, listening

26

to the team's comments. A discussion began about the new procedure for liaison between Accounting and Asset Management, and the schedule that had been drawn up for completing their investigations. There were concerns, particularly, about the schedule, but nothing that might have prompted him to leave the meeting. In the middle of the conversation Don simply got up, excused himself, and went out.

What did they think he was doing?

Popping out to the lavatory, they thought. He murmured, 'Excuse me a moment,' or 'Just a minute,' something like that. There was a clear implication that he would be returning almost immediately.

Could he have been going to fetch something from his office? Or to catch a passing colleague? Had he suddenly brought to mind a forgotten task? Or just lost track of time?

Don never lost track of time, they said, he was punctilious in that regard. Nor did he act as if he'd forgotten something or wanted to catch someone passing; he simply, calmly, walked out of the conference room. His secretary (who died the following year) at her desk just outside his office didn't see him. No one saw him except, it turned out, the receptionist downstairs, who noticed him leaving the building fifteen minutes later, at two thirty. The internal security camera confirmed it: he'd calmly walked past her and out of the main doors. I'd seen this footage already. Don has nothing with him, no bag, no coat. He doesn't seem to be in a hurry. There is no particular expression on his face. Just before he reaches the doors he puts his hand on the small of his back.

What had he been doing for those fifteen minutes, I asked them? It takes less than five to reach the main doors from the boardroom: I'd timed it as I came up.

They had not thought of this. They had no idea.

Had anything happened to prompt his sudden departure, a telephone call for instance? Had he been looking through his notes? Did he check his watch?

No phone call certainly; they would have remembered that. Rachel thought that Don's phone and watch had been on the table in front of him, he had a habit of putting them on a table or desk in front of him when making any sort of public address, but she didn't remember him paying them any attention while the meeting was going on. Obviously he must have taken them with him when he left the room: his phone was found in the bag at the Haven Hotel, and I already knew that there was nothing on it – call or voicemail or text – to offer any explanation for his behaviour. Assuming he was coming straight back, his colleagues had carried on talking, for perhaps as long as twenty minutes, before eventually breaking up the meeting. Although they had been puzzled, they assumed Don had been accosted by someone outside the meeting and held up. It was a time when senior managers were always being pulled into new meetings. They dispersed. It wasn't until 3.30 p.m., when Don was due in another meeting, that his secretary was asked to locate him, and it was another hour before they decided he must have gone home. They assumed at that point he'd been feeling unwell. At five o'clock his secretary left a message for Mrs Bayliss, saying that she hoped Don had got home all right and was feeling okay. As I knew from the file, Mrs Bayliss had been in council meetings until late that evening and didn't get it until nearly midnight. She immediately contacted the police and they instigated their search procedures, though by this time it was the early hours of the morning and there was a limited amount they could do. It wasn't until the Haven Hotel called the following morning to report the bag left on their ledge, that the investigation got properly under way.

I asked then about the sort of man Don was. Trevor, from HR, had known him the longest. He said that Don was old-school, a throwback, an absolute stickler for correct behaviour but decent and considerate.

'Kindly. Looked after his staff. He was first-aider in the department and you could go to him with absolutely anything, a headache or a splinter even, and he'd always take the time to help you.'

Perhaps, Trevor went on, some people thought him lacking in energy, not exciting enough, but his temperament was perfectly suited to his role. He was an accountant, after all, not a speculator. Rachel and Felix both agreed. As their manager, Don had been very supportive, almost avuncular, while insisting on high standards.

Had anyone disliked him?

On the contrary. Occasionally, someone made fun of his unprepossessing appearance, his paunch, his shambling walk, his dull suits, but never with malice. Recently, he'd spent some time in the Marshall Worth gym trying to sweat out a cold – a pitiful sight – and there were some snide comments about the sight of him in his old-style tracksuit as he slogged away on an exercise bike. But there was no one – absolutely no one – who hadn't been upset by what had happened.

Had they been surprised by the thought he'd taken his own life?

At first, absolutely. Don was undemonstrative, he'd given no signs of distress, yet in retrospect that explained only their initial surprise. Though he soaked up work without complaining, the pressure on him as senior manager had been extreme. They agreed that he'd always felt a strong sense of responsibility for his staff; later, in fact, they found out that there had been plans to relocate the entire accounting function from the UK to the US: for months only Don had stood against the move. He'd been working long hours, undoubtedly his health had suffered. There was that cold, that persistent cough.

I asked if he'd ever given the impression he was unhappy at home and they looked at me in surprise. No, he'd never talked about home. In fact, he never talked about himself.

I was due to talk to the CEO; indeed, I was already late. Rachel came with me out into the corridor. She wanted to say something more personal. It had been very hard for her to accept that Don had taken his own life, she said, he was the only person she'd ever known who had done so, it was impossible not to ask herself why he'd done it, and she had often wondered if she and his other colleagues had somehow, unwittingly, contributed to his despair or failed him in some way. Was there something they could have done to prevent him taking that awful step? For many years this had been an upsetting question in her mind. But, more recently, she'd remembered something which made her reconsider. One day, long before the crash – during Marshall Worth's boom years, when the company mood had been very buoyant – she'd gone into the hospitality suite to get some coffees and found Don there weeping on his own.

I asked her where the hospitality suite was and she

pushed open the door next to us, revealing a corporate lounge furnished with practical though probably not inexpensive sofas and easy chairs. Down one wall was a long table laid out with cups and saucers, glasses and plates, a coffee machine and bottles of soft drinks. Beyond were glass-fronted fridges containing beers, wine and so on. In the far corner was a table covered with newspapers and magazines next to a cabinet containing photographs of Marshall Worth dignitaries and various business events, award ceremonies, gala dinners and so on. Over there, Rachel told me, in that corner, that's where Don was standing, just crying. It was the quietness of it that had particularly struck her. It wasn't angry crying, or bitter, or even very distressed. It was oddly calm, in fact, as if his grief or melancholy were simply a part of him, like his baldness or his paunch, a function of who he was. As soon as he saw her, he began to make his way out of the room, not in any dramatic way but in the same calm manner, just quietly leaving, his slack, pale face wet with tears. Recalling this moment had made her feel that it hadn't only been work pressures that had pushed Don to take his own life, but, more profoundly, some sorrow he had been living with for a long time or that was a permanent part of him. Of course, she added, she had no idea what that sorrow was or why it was in him, and indeed she was only telling me what she felt, she didn't pretend she had any real insights, she'd hardly known him, she only hoped to add a little to the impressions I was gathering, and admittedly, she said, to try to finally come to terms with the inexplicable death of a man who had always been so supportive to her and who, in fact, she had more or less regarded as a father figure.

It was interesting, this image of a temperamentally melancholy man. I thought of the disc of Erik Satie's *Gymnopédies* which I'd found among Don's home office things and could imagine him one of those people whose innate sense of sadness is easily engaged. I asked if, by any chance, Rachel remembered what day she had seen Don there?

She shook her head. But she thought for a moment and said that she had been fetching coffees for a meeting with a visitor from the Financial Conduct Authority, and she remembered that because, as it happened, she discovered that they were both going to *The Secret Policeman's Ball* charity event the next day in London – when, purely by chance, they saw each other again. But, she went on, to make sure I didn't misunderstand her, the point she wanted to make – and this was just her feeling – was that Don's sorrow wasn't linked to *anything* in particular but was in fact a part of who he was, something he was able to hide most of the time, which came out at private moments.

'I still miss him,' she said. 'I miss his calmness. He was a good, good man.'

She turned away then, back to the others, and I went out and made my way towards the elevator, where I met my minder, who told me she'd just received a message from another member of staff who wanted to see me. There was no time before my meeting with the CEO, unfortunately, so I asked her to take some contact details, and proceeded as quickly as I could to the floor above.

Jack Polizzotti was a young fifty, grey but fit, trim in chinos and polo shirt; he looked as if he'd just come from his squash club. He gave me a warm greeting, tapped his watch and told me with an apologetic smile that he had only ten minutes before a transatlantic call came in.

His PA presented me with a non-disclosure form to sign.

'Sit, sit,' he said, gesturing energetically. Ten minutes was enough time for him to tell me everything he knew about Don Bayliss. Jack was one of those people who have no resting face: it was always animated. He hadn't known Don personally, he said, never met him, he'd arrived at the company three years after Don's disappearance, but his assistant had researched the historical records and he had himself looked into Don's top-level HR file. What he had to tell me, he said, was commercially sensitive and needed to remain completely confidential, but with that proviso he had no problem outlining Don's career at Marshall Worth.

Don had joined the company as a junior clerk shortly after the Bournemouth office was established in 1986. From the beginning, he was well-liked, a conscientious and capable member of staff. He had progressed steadily until his appointment as Head of Accounts twelve years later, the result of the patient acquisition of skills and experience, a textbook achievement of exemplary service.

'Until the May of that final year,' he added.

I looked at him.

'Then it all went pear-shaped for Don, I'm afraid.'

'Pear-shaped?'

'He was being investigated for financial wrongdoing.'

Jack allowed himself a wry smile. He could tell from my expression that I was surprised. He'd been surprised himself, he said. No one else at Marshall Worth knew anything about it, the file in his hand was the only record of it.

I asked if Don had known he was being investigated.

He had. In the file were written depositions from him. Disciplinary measures had been put in place, temporary restriction of privileges, withdrawal of various operational permissions. And suspension of salary, pending an outcome. Don had not been paid anything since the May of 2008. More than anything, Jack added, suspension of salary was a sign that the charge against Don was serious – embezzlement, in effect – and, at the time of Don's disappearance, the likelihood of a negative verdict was high.

I asked how much money was involved.

'Let's just say it was more than a mill and less than five. Over three to seven years.'

He glanced at his phone. He wished he could tell me more, but there were no more details available to him. In terms of corporate memory, he said, it was a long time ago and it belonged to a dark period most people at Marshall Worth would prefer to forget.

I commented that, although I knew little about the finance world, it seemed strange that Don should remain in post, unpaid, coming to work every day as if nothing was happening, working hard, doing his best to look after his staff, while such serious allegations against him were being pursued. Jack agreed. But what I had to remember was the strangeness of the time. It had been an absolutely existential crisis, not just for Marshall Worth, for everyone. Frankly, no one had known how much bad debt was in the system. Politicians were in no mood to cut anyone any slack: even the suspicion of an internal investigation into serious financial mismanagement could have brought the politicos down on them. So it seemed understandable to Jack that the senior guys in New York had proposed a procedure which might have been strange, was certainly unorthodox, but which ticked the necessary boxes: avoidance of scrutiny, impression of plausibility and the option of deniability. It was essential to keep it all quiet. Full disciplinary measures against Don kicked in straight away so that if wrongdoing were proved later they could say they'd acted at once. But, in the meantime, full discretion for Don so that no one need know about the issue, the regulatory authorities need not be informed; and if, in the end, Don's innocence was proved, his suspended salary could be backdated, it would be as if it had never happened, and, as a nice personal touch, his reputation would be safe. Don had agreed. With the exception of the CEO at the time, no one in the UK office had any idea what was going on, certainly none of Don's colleagues. Then, of course, Don took his own life and the inquiry was quietly closed down.

'They didn't reach a conclusion?'

'They moved on. To them, it was a few million unaccounted for offshore. Their focus was on tens of billions gone missing at home. As I say, they were desperate times.'

He looked at the phone again, then his watch; he had to let me go. He was sorry to have given me this news.

I asked if he thought Don was guilty.

He hesitated. He'd need to talk to the folks in New York. Sol Abramowitz in the Manhattan office was the guy with the information. All Jack had seen were redacted summaries of interviews and interim reports. The case seemed to have rested on many different assumptions. It looked to him as if Don had at least been guilty of making mistakes but, then again, he said, it had been such a weird time, frankly unorthodox things were being done.

'Looked at in the round,' he said, 'I think Don was a good guy. You'll have discovered that his staff adored him.'

He walked me to the door of his office.

'But then,' he said with a sigh, 'good guys sometimes do bad things.'

His PA came past me to hand Jack some papers, which he began to read instantly on his way back to his desk, his face showing complete concentration, as he shifted attention from old scandals to present matters, and I walked the other way, out of his office, to the elevator and out of the building on my way to the seafront. It was a longish walk but it would give me time in which to consider the new questions, not least why Don would want such a large amount of money, and what might have happened to it.

The East Cliff Café is situated on the promenade fifty metres east of Bournemouth Pier between a fish and chip restaurant and the public toilets. A typical English seaside café. By the door there's a glass-fronted counter stocked with pastries and buns, and, along the opposite wall, a row of booths, and I sat in the one at the back, where Don Bayliss had been sitting when Gregory Barrett saw him on the afternoon of his disappearance. I had some time to kill before Gregory arrived and I called Louise's department and asked for some financial checks to be run on the Bayliss accounts, and sat there with my coffee, thinking about Don's personal lack of ostentation, of the lavish splendour of his house, and the various differences between a man wanting to kill himself and a man wanting to save himself.

In some respects, I thought, they would behave the same way; they would in both cases contemplate extreme measures.

The café was busy with children on their half-term holiday and loud with the noise of their chatter, the coffee machines hissing and steaming, the thick white crockery clattering, the waitress calling out orders. After a while Gregory arrived, a short, neat man with a close-fitting grey beard dressed in black slacks and black turtle-neck sweater. He was the owner of Gregory's Hair and Beauty salon at Canford Cliffs, where both Don and his wife – Gregory called her Sylvia – were clients for many years.

I asked him to describe what had happened that October afternoon.

He'd been unwell and had stayed at home. Later in the day, feeling a little better, he'd taken Zhivago, his Afghan hound, for a walk along the front, and at three thirty had stopped at the café to pick up a latte. It was a cool and cloudy autumnal day, the last week of the season, and the café was empty, except for Don sitting at the back, and Gregory saw him straight away and naturally went over to say hello. Don had seemed disconcerted, as if Gregory was intruding, though Don was obviously on his own and didn't seem to be doing anything. It was a surprise to find him there in the middle of the afternoon of a weekday, and

Gregory had said something like 'You ill as well?', which is when Don had said, 'Don't worry about me, *I'm* all right.' His tone was almost belligerent, Gregory said. Certainly anti-social. Very un-Don-like. In fact, he'd seemed confused, or not exactly confused but lost in himself, like someone recently woken and still coming to consciousness. Gregory had explained to Don that he was taking a day off work because he was unwell but Don just stared. Occasionally he made murmuring noises but said nothing. There were a few moments of awkward silence. Then Gregory's coffee order was called out, with relief he said goodbye, and left Don there with that look of aggrieved bewilderment still on his face. The encounter had been so peculiar, Gregory said, that when he got home he said to his partner Sebastian, 'I think Don's losing it.'

I asked him if he thought Don had in fact committed suicide, as the inquiry had tentatively suggested, and Gregory said he had no doubt. Looking back, Don's black mood and disorientation seemed to be that of a man in extremity. He put it down to the pressure Don was under at work. Every week, it seemed, there was a piece in the paper about Marshall Worth closing its Bournemouth office and making everyone redundant. They sounded to Gregory like ruthless people. Did he think of Don as a sad person? No, Gregory said, not a depressive type, not emotionally unstable in any way but, on the contrary, very steady, always on a level. In fact, he had always seemed to Gregory one of those undemonstrative people who are quietly contented without really trying. Self-contained. 'He didn't ever say much, it's true. But he didn't seem to feel the need.' Gregory liked to divide his customers into the talkers and the non-talkers, and Don was firmly in the latter category.

'And his wife?'

He laughed. 'Sylvia's delightful, one of my favourites. But honestly, when she starts, you can't get a word in edgeways.'

He confessed that, from time to time, he'd wondered what their marriage was like, they seemed such opposites, she so outgoing, wearing her heart on her sleeve, he so quiet and mild. But they were so obviously happy. Perhaps, he said, the fact that they were opposites was their attraction for each other; people are difficult to fathom, thank God, the world would be a lot duller otherwise.

I asked him to say a few more words about the awkwardness he'd felt with Don in the café. Recollected emotion often triggers memory of specific details. And, in fact, there was something Gregory hadn't mentioned: he'd actually been a little annoyed with Don that day. Frankly, he'd suspected Don had recently decided to take his custom to another salon: at his last appointment, some months earlier, unusually, he'd declined to book another. Afterwards, of course, Gregory had seen it differently: Don must have been thinking he wouldn't be around for another haircut. Typical of an accountant – and odd, and appalling – to think ahead like that, to take into account your own suicide, and make the necessary adjustment in your schedule. In fact, Gregory went on, it was frightening to think how, perhaps for months, Don may have lived with the plan of ending his life. This idea, of Don going through his usual routines, going to work, eating dinner with Sylvia, never letting on, all the time nursing the terrible idea of destroying himself, haunted Gregory. What would that knowledge of impending self-destruction have done to Don? He must have been in a state of agony. No wonder he was behaving so oddly in the café: he was drinking his last coffee! It was the closest Gregory had ever come to pure and hopeless misery. Without knowing it, he'd been witness to something terrible. And he wondered now if he'd sensed it at the time. Perhaps that's what his feeling of awkwardness actually was, he said, his subconscious awareness of Don's misery, as if, without knowing it, he'd been picking up tiny little signals of Don's intention to kill himself, the way certain dogs sense cancers in people. In fact, he said, since that encounter he'd become aware of whole areas of experience which he had never thought about before, past lives, for instance, the existence of auras. Spiritual things. The tragedy of Don's death had opened Gregory's eyes to new realities of spirituality. But anyway, he said, he would never forget the sight of Don, sitting there with his cup of coffee, looking bewildered, acting strangely, stunned, no doubt, by the certainty of what he was about to do.

I waited a moment for the drama of this to die away. Then I pointed out that it was curious Don had been so quick to tell Gregory he was all right. Gregory thought this proved his point. Don obviously hadn't meant it, had spoken automatically, as if quoting a line from a movie. It was almost comical, in fact: he couldn't have sounded less all right if he'd tried. Or looked less all right, he added. 'Don't even ask me what his hair was like.'

I asked if it was possible there might have been a more prosaic reason for Don being in the café. That he was waiting for someone, for instance. Gregory had considered that possibility and had dismissed it. As I was doubtless aware, a waiting person shows a hundred different signs of expectation, little details, an alertness, an impatience, a readiness, checking their watch, peering out of the window, glancing towards the door. Don gave no such signs, he said.

I asked if Don had been wearing a watch. Gregory didn't know, he couldn't remember, but that wasn't the point.

Perhaps, I suggested, Don had just finished meeting someone.

Gregory had also considered that. He thought it unlikely. He'd noticed when he arrived that Don had already finished his coffee. Why would he stay on? What was he waiting for, sitting there on his own?

We'd finished our own coffees by now and it was time to go: there were families waiting for our table. It was late afternoon. The sun was soft and rich on the esplanade, and I watched him go away through the relentless holiday crowd, then I turned and walked in the opposite direction, back towards the Ventry Arms.

The dining room was full that night. At the far side, the New Zealander was sitting alone and when she saw me she lifted her hand in recognition and raised the copy of a book which she was reading and I lifted my copy of *Jekyll and Hyde* in return. It wasn't quite an invitation to join her, but it was friendly, and as I was deciding whether or not to go across to her, a waitress appeared at my shoulder. There was someone asking to see me, she said.

I said I wasn't expecting anyone.

It's a lady, the waitress told me, who didn't want to give her name.

I went with her into the lounge and there found a small

woman with a mass of frizzy hair and enormous glasses which enlarged her eyes and gave her an astonished expression. Her name, she said, was Mandy Roberts, which wouldn't mean anything to me, but she worked at Marshall Worth and had tried to see me earlier in the day, when I'd unfortunately been too busy. She was about to go travelling for a month, departing the following morning, but she wanted very much to speak to me, so she'd been forward enough to find out from Marshall Worth where I was staying and had come round in the hope that I might be able to give her just a few minutes. She was nervous, looking around as if fearing that someone was going to come in and find her there.

We sat together in armchairs in the bay window and she began by explaining that during the initial investigation she'd been in the US and had missed the opportunity to talk to the police at that time. Then she hesitated, as if unsure how to begin. She seemed, in fact, to be on the verge of tears.

After a moment, to get her started, I asked her if she'd worked with Don.

No, she said.

Had she been friendly with him?

No, she said emphatically. She'd only spoken to him once, in fact, the day before he disappeared. She began to twist her hair in her fingers.

I explained that everything she told me would remain confidential.

'The thing is, everyone said what a nice man he was.'

It was clear from the bitterness of her tone that her view of Don Bayliss was going to be different from those of the other people I'd already talked to.

At last she began to explain. She'd been eighteen years old and young for her age, rather nervous by nature, a late developer, as she put it, both emotionally and physically. It was her first job, she was just three months into it, coming to the end of her probationary period and feeling anxious. All the talk was of mass redundancies. She'd been in the little kitchen near her office when Don Bayliss came in. She'd never talked to him before, he worked on the floor above, but she knew he was very senior, and, to her alarm, she sensed at once that he'd come looking for her. Certainly he had no reason to be on her floor, and he was staring at her oddly. Closing the door behind him, he came very near, grinning or, as she put it, 'showing his teeth', and without introducing himself started with the sort of leering comments familiar to almost all young women unfortunate to find themselves alone with a certain type of older man, telling her how he couldn't help noticing how fit she was, how trim, how did she manage it? She was petrified, of course, and disgusted. He was old enough to be her father.

Talking all the time in a quiet mumble, subjecting her to a lengthy, incoherent stream of compliments, vacuous comments, meaningless questions, all the time peering at her lasciviously, he edged closer and closer, and soon he was standing so close she was sure he was going to touch her. 'Please,' she'd said. 'Oh please don't.' That seemed to throw him off. He gabbled some more random things, all the time looking at her pleadingly, as if, somehow, he expected her to help him out, to understand what he was after, to sympathise perhaps; then he suddenly seemed to lose confidence and he rushed out and she never saw him again.

'He was a predator,' she said. 'I'm sorry to say it.'

She was trembling. It was Don's manner that had alarmed her more than anything. He'd been so blatant in hitting on her and at the same time so incoherent it seemed he couldn't control himself or didn't really know what he was doing. It would have been less frightening, she said, if he'd been smooth and practised. His awkwardness made him appear unpredictable and in fact out of control; she actually wondered if he might force himself on her then and there in the kitchen.

It had cost her a lot to say all this and I thanked her. She wiped her eyes. She was sorry, she said, to offer nothing but negative thoughts about a man she hadn't known, but it had been important to her to give me her truth. I said I valued it. Indeed, I said, I was anxious not to miss anything she could tell me, and although the last thing I wanted was to make her relive her ordeal, I wondered if she remembered any other details of their unpleasant encounter, no matter how small, which might throw light on what had happened to Don. There was something, she said, a moment trivial in itself but in a way worse than the others. He said something that made her realise that he'd actually been watching her outside work. She belonged to a cycling club, and the previous weekend she'd cycled with them out to Hamworthy. To her horror, Don asked how it had been for her, and how long it had taken. Hamworthy was her favourite ride at the time and she thought at once she would never be able to cycle there again without thinking of Bayliss. She tried to ignore him but he'd persisted with his question and eventually she gabbled out an answer and, of course, he had nothing to say in reply, a sort of emptiness came into his face and his eyes glazed over; and immediately afterwards he bolted. She took off her glasses and her eyes were small and wet, and I reached over and took her hand and we sat together in silence, and at that moment the New Zealander came through the lounge from the dining room, carrying her book. Noticing me there, she smiled and changed direction but when she saw Mandy weeping next to me, my hand in hers, she turned away again in embarrassment and disappeared up the stairs.

It had been such a horrible experience, Mandy went on between sobs, and the next day he'd gone and killed himself and after that she felt guilty thinking badly of him, and felt also – as many victims of such approaches do – that it was all somehow her fault, that she'd misunderstood him, that he was actually a vulnerable man who needed help not rejection. But he hadn't seemed vulnerable, she said fiercely, on the contrary, he'd absolutely seemed predatory, an old man with all the authority of his seniority, clumsy, inconsiderate, with no care at all for the feelings of a powerless young woman new in the job and still finding her way in life.

Her feelings were very understandable and I thanked her again for taking the brave decision to talk to me about such a traumatic event, and waited with her until she was calm again. She was grateful to me, she said, for allowing her to speak. It had been a weight on her mind all these years. Now, perhaps, she could move on. Did I have any more questions?

Only one, I said. How long does it actually take to cycle to Hamworthy?

She gave me a look, as if she suspected I wasn't taking her seriously.

'From here?'

'From Parkstone, say.'

'About three-quarters of an hour,' she said. I thanked her again and said that I hoped she enjoyed her travels, and she got to her feet and said goodbye, and I went with my copy of *Jekyll and Hyde* into the dining room which was now nearly deserted.

The New Zealander was no longer around but coincidentally I was placed at the table where she had been sitting. I had the lamb and the gooseberry fool, and thought about the many things I'd learned that day. I wondered what effect the Marshall Worth investigation might have had on Don Bayliss's mental health. I thought about the fact that he hadn't been paid for five months, and about his expensively appointed house, and about Mrs Bayliss and her view of her husband. I considered Gregory, for whom, in retrospect, Don had become a terrifying *memento mori*. I thought about Don's loyal and admiring colleagues and, of course, about Mandy, whom Don had traumatised so badly. In my mind Don had never been very sharply defined; now, he was slipping even further out of focus. I couldn't read him. In truth, he seemed an unlikely embezzler and an unlikely predator. But he seemed an unlikely anything.

When my coffee arrived I turned to *Jekyll and Hyde*.

Stevenson's 'shilling shocker', which is how he described it, is self-evidently a story of opposites; they're everywhere, in fact, even in the most incidental narrative details: clear light of day one moment, an appalling fog the next; a smart front door with well-polished brass plate next to one which showed 'prolonged and sordid negligence'; Utterson's drily courteous manner in dialogue with Hyde's 'unfitting' language. Contrasting rooms are important too; one minute we're in the richly appointed studies of lawyers and doctors, and the next in Jekyll's distasteful and dingy dissecting rooms. Such details seem disquieting reflections of the ultimate opposition at the heart of the story, of good and evil, not good and evil next to each other, however, but, more terrible still, one inside the other, Hyde lurking inside Jekyll.

I thought again of Don Bayliss. Did he live with some nameless sorrow or was he quietly contented? Was he avuncular or predatory? An old-school sticker for the rules or a calculating embezzler? I did not, in fact, believe in any of these Don Baylisses. I reviewed the various reasons for killing oneself, intolerable pain, say, or confusion, fear, guilt, self-sacrifice, and felt that I knew nothing about Don Bayliss's reason for killing himself, for all these reasons might fit or none at all. Then an anecdote came into my mind about Erik Satie, another diffident man whose music

Don played in his home office. Pathologically shy, Satie was afraid of drawing attention to himself, but sometimes his very shyness led him to do outrageous things. Once, at a party in a wealthy patron's grand house, he badly needed the lavatory but was too shy to ask where it was, so he slipped out of the drawing room to try to find it on his own, but couldn't, and, roaming round the house, became more and more desperate until at last, finding himself on the lawn directly outside the drawing room, he could stand it no longer and urinated on the grass in full view of everyone inside. Sometimes, I thought, the exhibitionist bursts out from inside the introvert.

At last I put Don Bayliss from my mind and went back to *Jekyll and Hyde*, paying more attention this time to Mervyn Peake's illustrations, after the New Zealander's comments the previous night; and one drawing in particular caught my eye, a street scene at night, a tiny, almost insignificant, overcoated Hyde casting an enormous shadow up a vast windowless wall. I read until nine thirty, then went up to my room to get an early night before my morning visit the next day to Belmarsh Prison.

The Category A prison is in Woolwich, not far from the river, a complex of long, low buildings, all concrete and wire, more like a military installation than a prison. At its heart is the HSU – High Security Unit – a prison within a prison, by reputation the most secure facility in the country, where, over the years, a number of high-profile offenders – you might even call them celebrities – have been detained. It's here that Dwight Fricker was currently being held.

He'd been involved in an attack on two guards. It wasn't the first time. Throughout his incarceration he'd been repeatedly involved in violent incidents. Belmarsh was only the latest prison to hold him; previously, he had been in Hull, Wandsworth, Wormwood Scrubs, Broadmoor and Ashworth Hospital, where he underwent a course of intensive therapy and medication. He once described himself as a 'a businessman with an interest in fine art who occasionally loses it'. Indeed, for years he'd run various businesses – clubs, strip joints, table-dancing bars, and, on the side, illegal activities such as extortion and blackmail – and in his spare time collected paintings, specialising in works known as 'art brut', but he'd always been known for his violent, perhaps psychopathic temper, and had received his life sentence for the murder of a young woman employed at one of his clubs. A few days after she was reported missing, she'd been found in the river near the Dartford Crossing minus her arms. I'd seen photographs of him. He was always dressed in black – black shirt, black trousers – with a discreet splash of gold jewellery. His head was shaved.

On the day I arrived to see him, Fricker had just completed a week's solitary in Special Cell 02, punishment for inciting a small riot. I was told he was calm again and had readily agreed to see me.

'He don't get many visitors,' the officer told me as we went along the metal walkway to the visitors' room. 'If he's in a good mood, he'll want to talk to you about painting.' Apparently Fricker himself painted, huge canvases of crude daubs he described as 'Outsider Art'. 'They tell me it's a thing,' the officer said. 'He's certainly an outsider. Outside all that's sane. But he can talk, I'll give him that.'

Fricker was seated at the table when we went in. I told the officer I'd be happier if we were left alone but he had instructions to wait at the back of the room. Overhearing this, Fricker laughed but said nothing. He was forty-five years old, in good shape, with a large, rock-like head, all hard lines and flat planes, and deep-set eyes, very dark in colour. His hands, which he rested unmoving on the tabletop, were enormous, scarred and scabbed. He looked at me for some time without speaking, and I looked back, and after a while, I slid the card which Mrs Bayliss had found across the table, and he glanced at it and returned his gaze to me.

'Heard of William Kurelek?' he asked. His voice was abrasive.

I shook my head.

'Did his best work not far from here. The Maudsley. Psychiatric hospital, South London. Rats,' he added. 'The rat spirit. Open the skull, let it out.'

He glanced again at the card.

'Piss-poor design,' he said. 'Wrong colour. Shoddy. Our pasts,' he said, 'all shoddy. Art helps us make sense of it.'

I asked him if he remembered someone called Donald Bayliss.

He stared at me, shook his head. 'Who is he?'

I told him Don had gone missing, and that one of Fricker's

56

cards had been found in his possession. He shrugged. I asked him how Don might have got hold of it and he made no answer. 'I heard once Emile Montale had a card of mine,' he said after a while. 'They found it on him after he died. I'd never liked his stuff but it made me look again.'

I asked him if he'd changed his mind about it and he shook his head. 'Not honest work. Honesty's the only thing in art. Almost impossible to achieve. Klee, Dubuffet, the mainstream guys, just pretty. Kurelek has it, Kurelek was honest. What about this Bayliss? Did he have it?'

I explained that he had been an accountant not an artist but Fricker showed no interest, looking at me patiently. All this time he hadn't moved his hands, not once, they lay in front of him, totally inert, heaps of bone and gristle.

'They say I don't like people. I love people, fucking love them. It's just, they can't be honest. That's what I'm saying in my paintings, what I'm trying to tell them.'

I asked him what he was going to do when he got out. It wasn't in fact clear that he would ever get out, his behaviour inside had been too chaotic, but the future always has a powerful hold on those incarcerated, as it does on all of us, of course. Was he thinking of spending more time painting?

He said it would be difficult. He had a number of business interests, which would require his attention.

I asked about the accountants who worked in his

businesses and he considered me again in that still, unblinking way.

'This Bayliss of yours,' he said. 'I don't remember him.'

I described him in more detail.

Fricker nodded. 'There was a time, fifteen, twenty years ago, I was looking for a straight accountant. Someone with a pedigree. The books needed – what shall I say – *sanitising*.' He smiled, revealing dark gaps in his mouth where teeth were missing. 'My people put some feelers out. It's possible he came to me then.'

I asked if it were possible that Don had actually worked for him.

'Possible,' he said. 'My people would have handled it, set him up, put him on the payroll. Most people,' he went on seamlessly, 'are fantasists. They're blind, blind to the terror, to the horror, that's why we need artists, honest artists. Of course,' he said, 'they shit on us, the fantasists. You know the only person understands me?'

I shook my head.

'My wife.'

As he said it he moved his hands for the first time, turning them over, palms up, making an ambiguous gesture, a cupping or an expression of emptiness, perhaps the nearest thing he could imagine to honesty.

'Fuck off now,' he said mildly. 'Fuck off back to the other

fantasists. Tell them about my work,' he added. 'Tell them to put their noses in it.'

He lifted his big face towards the officer at the back of the room, who stepped forward immediately, and my interview with Dwight Fricker was over.

I was careful not to sensationalise it when I went to see Sylvia later that day. I told her about Fricker's casual remark that he'd been looking for a 'straight accountant' in the period before Don disappeared, but made it clear to her that he genuinely seemed to have no idea who Don was. I didn't believe he'd ever had any personal contact with him. If she was frustrated by this lack of development, she didn't show it. As she'd told me herself, she was a practical person capable of thinking through issues in a calm and methodical manner, and she asked me a number of questions about my conversation in Belmarsh, all very reasonable but unproductive, and the discussion eventually petered out. The only time she showed emotion – her voice cracking as she spoke – was when we discussed the possibility of Don still being alive. I had to tell her I did not believe the existence of Fricker's card in Don's possession made it any more or any less likely. But, I went on, some new information had come to light which might change the picture, and I asked her if she knew that Don was being investigated by Marshall Worth for alleged embezzlement.

She was a woman, I knew, who could handle direct questions, but for the first time she found nothing to say and for several seconds stared at me unblinking, her mouth a little crooked. She was so shocked, in fact, that she forgot to deny the possibility of it. Soon I could see anger building in her, her face becoming congested, but she mastered her emotion and when she finally spoke she was in control of herself again.

She asked me for precise details and I explained that I was not able to give them to her. She asked who at Marshall Worth had made the accusation and what evidence they had and why she had not been informed and a number of other questions. She gestured round the lavish room, at the art works, the designer furniture, pointing out the Fyfields, the Amber Lewis, the enormous Christian Hetzel abstract above the mantelpiece. Perhaps someone at Marshall Worth had decided that Don couldn't afford all this. Well, he couldn't, she said. But she could, having inherited a large estate on the death of her father, who had owned extensive land in Norfolk. If anyone had serious accusations to make about their finances, she hoped they would make them in the usual way and allow her to present the relevant facts. It was an argument she was up for.

I told her that the allegation of embezzlement would

almost certainly never be formally raised. Nor was it certain to turn out to be a material factor in my investigation, I said, though I added that a connected issue might be.

'Yes?'

I told her that, as a result of the investigation, from the May of 2008 Don's salary had been suspended and I asked if she had noticed this at the time, and, if she had, what she thought the reason for the suspension had been.

Again she was quiet for a moment. This time she didn't question me, she simply told me that I was wrong: Don had received his salary as normal until after his disappearance. She remembered very clearly. Asking me to wait, she rose and went out to her office, where, she said, she would access the relevant information to prove her point. This information I already possessed, gathered for me by Louise's team, but I waited, and after about a quarter of an hour Sylvia reappeared with a strange expression on her face, which, again, I had expected. She told me her records showed that from May to October money had continued to be paid into their account – but not quite as normal. She had noticed, just now, that the amounts arriving in that period had been slightly different from the usual amounts, and moreover, she went on, they seemed to have arrived from a different source: the initials identifying it were not the familiar initials.

I asked what source it was.

She didn't know. Nor, in fact, did I. The monthly deposits were so similar to the usual amounts, and the identification numbers so close to the usual Marshall Worth identifiers, that everyone – including the original investigating police team at Bournemouth – had missed it. Everyone assumed that the payments had come from another division of the company. Was it possible they had come instead from one of Dwight Fricker's businesses? I did not ask this question, nor did Sylvia allude to it, though I wondered if she thought of it as she sat there looking at me.

In any case, by now I was late for my next appointment, and I took my leave of her.

It was nearly five o'clock and I was due to speak to Rose Seagrief. She had been Don's Alexander Technique teacher in London, though she was now retired and had moved to Bournemouth, coincidentally living nearby, on The Avenue. Throughout most of September and October 2008, she had seen Don each Wednesday evening, the final session taking place only a week before his disappearance.

It was another warm day and, as I strolled through the quiet lanes of comfortable Branksome Park, I felt, as before, the soothing effects of the soft afternoon sunshine, which patterned the greenery, behind which the mansions were generally invisible. From the pavement I saw only laurel hedges and rhododendron, occasionally a brief glimpse of sweeping drive, a portico, fountain spray, some gables. Everything here was discreet or, one might say, hidden, though thanks to gossip certain things were common knowledge: I passed a mock-colonial plantation house owned – I'd been told by the waitress at the Ventry Arms – by a former football manager, and a ranch-style bungalow where a well-known television personality lived. The real estate here was so valuable that the rich frequently bought up old houses, knocked them down and built something entirely new in their own preferred style.

The Avenue was the main drag from the Westbourne shops down to the front, and now, at the end of the afternoon, it was busy with cars coming up from the beach at Branksome Chine. Once nicknamed 'Millionaires' Row', it had been partly redeveloped with low-rise apartment blocks containing two- or three-bedroom flats for retirees, and it was in one of these that, after spending the whole of her life in South London, Rose now lived. She was sixty-seven years old, a loose-limbed woman in shapeless sweater with a smile full of gum, and a rescued border collie, Ella, just recovering from swallowing a football. This seemed improbable but she explained that the dog had punctured the ball first. Ella regarded us queasily from her basket in the kitchen.

We went through the living room to sit on the balcony where the last of the sun was coming through the top of a large magnolia tree. Leaving London had been the best thing she'd ever done, she said. In fact, she found it hard to believe she hadn't left earlier. Instead, she'd lived and worked all her adult life in a cramped flat in Elephant and Castle. It had been there that Don Bayliss had gone to see her with his bad back.

I asked about her work with Don.

He'd first suffered with his back when he was a young man working in the City; someone had recommended her to him; she'd fixed him, and after that he returned to her whenever he had a problem. Physical therapists were like dentists or hairdressers, she said; once you find one that suits you, you stick with them. So Don had stuck with her, even after he moved to Bournemouth. Whenever his back flared up he'd drive to Elephant and Castle at the end of the day to see her, stay the night in a West End hotel, then travel back down to Bournemouth early the next morning. Over the years she'd seen him many times.

I asked her to tell me a little about the format of her usual sessions.

To begin with, she would spend some time observing a client, to make sure of the specific problem; then there would be some posture-related activities; finally a period on the massage table for relaxation exercises. Don's usual problem was frozen shoulder, which happened when he was under pressure, basically his body's cry for help. He had a strong body, she said, but he bottled things up; it was always the same, the pressure would build until, in the end, his whole back would go into spasm. The key was to enable him to relax, to open up and let go.

And had he opened up?

Her clients always opened up, she said, a little evasively. She created the safe space they needed, the necessary atmosphere of trust. Lying on her table, under her hands, they were vulnerable, exposed, and yet open to their feelings and able to express them. It was not uncommon for them to weep.

I asked if Don had wept.

She looked askance and told me that there was such a thing as professional confidentiality. To that, I said I'd talked to the people at Marshall Worth and was aware of the issues at work, but she waved a dismissive hand. Of course, everyone knew about those. I waited. Confidentiality or not, mostly people want to speak: all they require is the silence in which to do it. After a moment she asked me if I'd known that Don had never wanted to be an accountant; he'd told her this not long after he first started going to her. He didn't even like working with numbers. 'He hated them,' she said.

I wondered why then he'd continued so long in his job.

'You'd need to ask that woman,' Rose said.

'You mean Sylvia?'

She merely turned away from me and looked across the balcony at the magnolia tree.

I asked her about those last sessions in 2008. Had Don opened up to her then?

She hesitated. 'I couldn't say.'

'But you remember the sessions?'

'Oh yes.'

Again, I waited in silence, and at last she spoke. Don had been uncharacteristically distressed.

The financial crisis, I said, was at its worst.

She dismissed this. Don was distracted, uneasy. He would lose track of what she was saying to him, bite his lip, scowl. He seemed . . . angry.

She hadn't mentioned any of this to the police at the time, as I pointed out to her, but she said that there was nothing she could have told them with any certainty, these were only her impressions, her intuitions, though, she added, she was rarely wrong in these matters, she was naturally very empathetic. But, anyway, when she was interviewed by the police, she'd still been hoping Don would return and wanted to avoid making assumptions which might embarrass him later.

I asked what assumptions they had been. She hesitated once more, then said in a rush, 'I thought: *He's done something he wishes he hadn't.*' All his scowls, she said, all his little groans and sighs, they seemed to her the familiar mannerisms of regret or guilt. He seemed angry with himself, she said, for something he'd done.

I thought about that.

After a while I said, 'Or something he *hadn't* done?'

'Yes,' she said after a moment. 'That's also possible.'

'Or something he was about to do,' I added.

We sat there. Her dog crept out to join us and lay down on the balcony next to Rose. She was glad she'd told me all this, she said. She felt she could speak about it because she knew that Don was not coming back. 'He's gone,' she said.

I asked her how she knew that.

Not long ago, she said, she'd dreamed about him. They were together in a party of Japanese tourists. A lot of Japanese come to Bournemouth. In this group, they went to visit an old tower on the clifftop at Alum Chine, which didn't exist in reality but in her dream was famous for its view. They went up in a lift, which tilted as it rose and everyone lay down on the floor except Don and Rose. Don smiled at her. He had such a kind smile, she said. Then they went into a room just below the top of the tower. There was a door to the roof and Rose fumbled for the door handle which wouldn't turn, she couldn't turn it, and Don came to stand next to her and said, 'I'll do it. I know how.' And then she woke.

She smiled shyly. 'He went through the door,' she said. 'He went through and he's not coming back.'

I thanked her for all this, including her dream. There was one final thing, I said, a logistical detail. The police had recorded all the dates of Don's overnight stays at the Piccadilly Hotel – four Wednesdays in September and another four Wednesdays in October – but they had not recorded the dates of her sessions with him, though presumably they were the same. Could she confirm?

She looked at my list and frowned. No, she said, the dates weren't right. She'd only seen Don a few times in September and not at all in October. She left the balcony and returned a few minutes later with an old appointments diary for 2008, in which she had written the dates of Don's sessions at the time. As she'd said, there weren't many, just the first three Wednesdays in September. She explained that Don had always responded quickly to her treatment and rarely needed more than two or three consecutive sessions.

'What he actually needed,' she added, 'was some therapy.' She'd told him so, in those last sessions. 'Perhaps,' she added, 'that's what he was doing in London on those other dates.'

'Perhaps,' I said.

She thought that must be it. Don had been a good man, she said, she could tell. A gentle man, kind. She had the impression he'd been a supportive manager at work, particularly good with younger members of staff. A protective, fatherly figure. She'd always felt it was a pity Don hadn't had children, he would have been a wonderful father, she said.

We parted at the door.

'If he had done something he regretted,' she said, 'I think it would have tormented him.'

I thanked her for her time, patted the dog, and left.

The Ventry Arms was quiet that evening, the dining room almost empty. I had the ragout of beef and some cheese and fruit, and reflected on the day. I wondered what Don had been doing on those five Wednesday evenings in London in September and October. Dwight Fricker was living in Holland Park at that time: did Don go to see him? I wondered too what Don could have done, or not done, or was going to do, that he felt guilty about. There were a number of obvious possibilities, not least the embezzlement, if it turned out to be true, and his imminent suicide, if that turned out to be true, but the obvious is not always the correct solution, and it seemed to me that Don was someone who did not do things, not someone who did.

I remembered too Dwight Fricker telling me in Belmarsh that honesty is almost impossible to achieve.

As usual, I had taken my copy of *Jekyll and Hyde* into the dining room but also two other things to read first.

I had picked up a leaflet at the tourist office at Hamworthy marina. It featured photographs of a busy harbour and the sparkling ocean decorated with white sails, and also several warnings about dangerous tides. Before going to see Mrs Bayliss, I'd taken a taxi out there, a scenic drive once we went beyond the conurbation of Poole and the ferry terminal, spacious roads round the shore of the harbour, on flat, sandy grasslands low-lying under an enormous marine sky. It would be a pleasant ride for cyclists, and easy, I thought, even for someone as out of condition as Don. There was a holiday park, then outdoor sports facilities, then thousands of brilliant white prefabricated holiday homes, all smart, clean and temporary, and finally, at the end of Napier Road, the marina itself, tucked against the mouth of the Rock Lea river – a notorious spot for suicides. There had been several there over the past few years.

As well as my leaflet, I had a printout of the front page story from the *Bournemouth Echo* of Friday, 13 October 2006, which Louise's team had located in the publishers' archives for me. This was the day before *The*

Secret Policeman's Ball in London, in other words the day when Rachel had encountered Don quietly weeping in the hospitality suite of Marshall Worth. Some people cry without a prompt, others require something to get them going. I knew from Sylvia that Don liked the local paper, it seemed probable that a new edition on the table where he had been standing would catch his eye. I studied it for a while. There was a photograph of a police van surrounded by angry women, some of them throwing missiles. In the van, under escort, had been Robert Ludlow, a thirty-five-year-old physics teacher recently dismissed from one of the local secondary schools. A month earlier he had eloped with a fourteen-year-old girl, one of his students, fleeing with her to France, where they checked into a family room in a Dieppe hotel as father and daughter, and at which, after a few days, they were apprehended and returned to England by the French authorities. Predictably, there had been outrage, made worse by Ludlow's steadfast refusal to express any regret and his insistence that he'd done nothing wrong, and complicated by the fact that the girl, Debbie Foxton, had gone on television to say that she intended to marry 'Mr Ludlow' as soon as legally possible. Was this something that might have made Don Bayliss cry?

I thought about this for a while, then, at last, putting both leaflet and printout aside, turned to *Jekyll and Hyde*.

Utterson the lawyer knows that Jekyll has recently altered his will in favour of Hyde. Alarmed, he resolves to try to find out more, and after a patient wait manages to accost Hyde at the door of Jekyll's old dissecting room. It's the first time in the story we've found ourselves face to face with the creature, and I was interested in Stevenson's description of him, which relies once more on oppositions and contradictions. Hyde is 'pale' but also 'flushed' with anger. He shrinks back with a frightened hiss but is soon on the front foot, snarling with savage laughter. He is in general a 'murderous mixture of timidity and boldness'. Yet none of this accounts for the instinctive disgust which Utterson feels. There is something else, something hidden, and Utterson thinks it must be what he calls a 'foul soul'.

Reading on, I had reached the passage describing Hyde's murder of Sir Danvers Carew when the New Zealander appeared in the dining room and, seeing me, came across. She was dressed as before in a tracksuit, rangy and lean and lightly sweating, and I asked if she had been for a run. No, she said, she'd been leading an aerobics class by video link for her class in Auckland. She was a fitness and yoga instructor, she explained, and, though she was meant to be on a holiday, she'd agreed to deliver a few classes online while she was away. We introduced ourselves; people called her 'Mac', she said. I asked her to join me, and we ordered coffees.

It was obvious at once that Mac was one of those people who are comfortable in their own skin, sitting at a loose angle to her chair to give her arms a chance to move around, which they did when her enthusiasm was engaged. From the beginning, she lacked reserve, looking at me steadily and appraisingly with her frank grey eyes, pointing her nose at me in what might have been a challenging way. There was a hint of mischief lurking in the corner of her mouth. She began mischievously, in fact, saying that she'd wanted to talk to me about *Jekyll and Hyde* the previous evening but didn't like to disturb me when it seemed, she said, looking at me with those cool eyes, that I had company.

Her tone implied a question which at first I hoped to answer with silence.

'You were having quite an effect on her,' she said, after a moment. I could hear the smile in her voice.

As carefully as I could, I said that the lady had become upset in remembering something that had happened to her many years earlier.

She thought about that.

'Friend of yours?'

I said I'd never met her before.

She looked at me then for a while longer. 'You a therapist?'

I said I wasn't.

'It's just you know how to make a total stranger cry.' Finally she laughed. 'You English,' she said. Her laugh made a beautiful sound.

I did not tell her that I'm not English. I asked her instead what she'd wanted to tell me about my book. She was, it turned out, a big fan of Stevenson and had read everything by him, including the minor books she described as 'fun trash', and liked it all, the perky early travel writing like *Travels with a Donkey in the Cévennes* as much as the grave, final, fragmentary *Weir of Hermiston*, which Stevenson was writing when he died, in Samoa, dropping dead literally in the middle of a sentence. But *Jekyll and Hyde* was her favourite, and she had read it several times. It was the reason she had decided to visit Bournemouth, to see the place where it was written. So we began to talk about the book. Thinking about the passages I'd just read which describe Hyde, I asked her what she thought it was that made the man so repulsive.

'He's small,' she said promptly. 'If he wasn't small he'd just be another ogre.'

That was interesting.

Obviously nasty too, she went on. But also, because of his size, vulnerable. Needy, in fact. His neediness made him much more than simply frightening, and also unpredictable;

74

like a small dog, he might whine and writhe, or he might suddenly take your hand off. Neediness is disgusting, she said.

'Though, of course,' she added, 'we all have needs.'

I reminded her of Utterson's theory of the 'foul soul' and she shrugged. 'Makes sense if you believe in souls.'

We talked then about other things, her career, her travelling. Every year, she liked to take most of the summer off, see something of the world, often going to places where her favourite writers had lived and worked. She'd been to Paris, to see the districts patrolled by Simenon's Inspector Maigret; and to Simla in northern India, where Kipling anatomised the ruling classes of the Raj; and to Lisbon, where the elusive Fernando Pessoa had lived, writing under many different pseudonyms, inventing whole biographies for his *noms de plume*, in fact, until he had hidden himself completely inside them. Naturally, all these places had changed, sometimes almost entirely, since they were described by these writers, but often there was something left untouched, a glimpse of the past, like the Lisbon street where Pessoa had lived, still unchanged and so dark and gloomy it had given her a sudden vivid feeling for the man, hunkered down in his writing, finding brilliant scraps in the bleakness.

I asked if she'd been to see the site of Stevenson's house.

She had, of course, and thought it ridiculously unassuming in a very English way, the little garden so modest it seemed fearful of drawing attention to itself. But she liked the chine at the end of it falling away into darkness, and liked to imagine the bohemian Stevenson living there, though she thought it odd that he should write *Jekyll and Hyde*, 'of all things', among the respectable folk of Bournemouth.

Or very natural, I pointed out. A case of secret lives, the disreputable hiding among the respectable, as so often.

'His wife was disreputable,' she said. 'Don't know about Stevenson himself. A bohemian, yes. But surely that's a different thing.'

We had finished our coffees and I began to excuse myself. She looked at me. I didn't say much about myself, did I, she said. I asked a lot of questions and answered none. After nearly an hour talking to me, she didn't know anything about me.

She asked if I were married.

I said that I wasn't.

She wasn't either. She asked me if I had children.

I told her I didn't. Was this an interrogation?

Yes, she said. Please answer honestly and succinctly. Where do you live?

I said I had forgotten.

Where do you come from?

Nowhere.

Are you rich?

In some things.

What do you do for a living?

I told her.

She looked at me curiously for a while. Going missing, she said at last, was, in her opinion, a common yearning. Who hasn't at some point dreamed of leaving things behind, starting a new, a better, life, some place where no one knows your secrets and your failures and your humiliations, where you can finally succeed, finally be the person you were meant to be?

She said it with such force I was taken aback and she asked me if I'd never felt that.

I said I wasn't sure, and her mouth moved in that humorous way. She didn't believe me, she said.

As I rose to go, she said she was going to return to Stevenson's memorial garden for a final look before flying back to New Zealand in a couple of days' time and suggested I join her; and I said I would like that very much; and she looked at me as she had before, with either curiosity or pity, I couldn't be sure which, and laughed again, making that beautiful sound.

I sat in my room thinking about the reasons why a man

might disappear. Mac was right, one reason might be to find oneself, to start again, to discard your old self. To make a change, or a statement. Or simply for practical reasons. To leave your home in Baghdad one day, as I had done many years earlier, and go to school in another country, begin to speak another language, go to work in yet another country, be called 'Finder' instead of Talib, find yourself in an English resort talking or not talking to a young woman from New Zealand about *Jekyll and Hyde*. I got up and stood at my window looking into the darkness, in the vague direction of Stevenson's vanished house, thinking about his disreputable wife, a woman who had lived in the Wild West of America, who rolled her own cigarettes and knew how to shoot a pistol, and who so scandalised the Bournemouth matrons all those years ago. And finally I thought about my own wife and son. For a long time after they died, I had their images in my mind all the time, there wasn't a waking moment when I didn't seem to see them in my memory; and at night I suffered the predictable nightmares. Then, after I left Paris and became a finder, their images gradually disappeared. At first it was a relief. But as the years have passed I long to have them fill my mind again. Mac had been partly right. I was living a new life. But it was not of my choosing, not a fresh start but an exile, with no possible return.

I stood there trying to hear again in my mind the noise Mac's laughter made but could not. Then I got into bed and lay there waiting for sleep.

Upper Parkstone in Poole is a residential sprawl of low-rise brick divided from the more prosperous Lower Parkstone by the A35. Streets of tightly packed houses run perpendicular to the main drag, Ashley Road, where the shops are located, the mini supermarkets, launderettes and nail bars; and Uppleby Road is one of these, a street of pebble-dash semis, new-build brick townhouses and, at the end, a small cottage plastered grey, lone survivor of an earlier period. It was here that Mr Entwhistle lived, and where, according to Mr Entwhistle, at five o'clock in the afternoon of 30 October 2008, a man resembling Don Bayliss had arrived to look at the bicycle he was selling.

The front door opened into the tiny living room and Mr Entwhistle sat me in an armchair against the back wall and brought me tea in a mug commemorating the Silver Jubilee of 1977. He was ninety years old, a small, badgery man wearing a cardigan out at the elbows, mild in manner and mild-faced, glasses with thick lenses perched on the end of his nose, which he lifted into the air, animal-like, at unpredictable moments, as if trying to pick up my scent. It wasn't clear from the way he peered around that he knew exactly where I was. It didn't matter, however. He talked to the room in a generous stream of words, as if the opportunity to talk came along only rarely.

He remembered the whole thing very well, he said. Naturally he did, because of what the poor man did to himself, though it was important, he said, to begin at the beginning, with the bicycle itself, or rather the advertisement about it that he'd placed in the local paper and also on a local website whose name he couldn't remember, a process he described in some detail, which muddled him for a while, though he got through it eventually to get on to the bicycle, for which he had clearly had a great deal of affection, telling me when he'd bought it and how much he'd paid for it, and what sort of condition it was in, and in this way, very slowly, he proceeded to the moment when Don had called round to see it.

I spoiled all this by asking him if he was certain that the man was actually Don Bayliss and he looked deflated and said, well, no, actually, not absolutely certain. He was an honest man and didn't want to mislead me. But when he'd seen the pictures of Don in the *Echo* a few days later he'd *felt* very strongly that it was the same man. A middle-aged man, he remembered that, though he remembered little else about Don's appearance, it was such a long time ago. In fact, I knew from his original statement in the police files that he'd never been able to remember much about the man who came to see his bicycle, not even whether he had been wearing a suit or if he was bald or not. Indeed, Mr Entwhistle had been frankly disbelieved by the original team. I asked him why he'd *felt* the man to be Don Bayliss, and he said after some thought that it just fitted: an educated man quietly spoken but jittery, nervous, as he would be if he was thinking of killing himself, who fled before he had a chance to fetch the bike for inspection, just as he would if he was having second thoughts about killing himself.

I said that in fact it was assumed that Don didn't in fact have second thoughts and he was again deflated.

I asked if the man had said what he wanted the bike for.

He couldn't remember.

Had he mentioned cycling out to Hamworthy?

What would he want to do that for, Mr Entwhistle wanted to know?

Had he mentioned working at Marshall Worth or living in Branksome Park?

No.

Did he sound depressed?

No. Just nervous.

Had he said anything at all to give him the impression that he was Donald Bayliss?

'No one believed me at the time,' Mr Entwhistle said sadly. 'And now you don't believe me either.'

I asked if the man had had a bad cough.

He stared in my direction for a long time. 'Yes,' he said at last, amazed. 'That's right.' He'd completely forgotten. Now he remembered. In fact, the cough had been so bad he'd asked the man if he was ill and he'd replied no, he wasn't, but while Mr Entwhistle was getting the bike from the shed at the back he was planning to advise the man he shouldn't ride it until he got better.

He was eager for me to believe him and sensed that I was starting to. It was such a shame, he said, that he couldn't remember more.

I asked him if the man had asked any questions about the bicycle. About its condition, perhaps, or how many gears it had, or did it come with a pump and lights. Mr Entwhistle thought about that. Yes, he said, the man had asked about lights, he was particular about that, and Mr Entwhistle had to say no, he didn't think so; and then, when he was fetching the bike he thought he'd been mistaken and perhaps it had lights after all, but it didn't matter, of course, because when he returned, the man had gone. He'd gone out into the street looking up and down for him, but in the end he'd just taken the bicycle back to the house and re-advertised it the next week, when someone, a man from Bournemouth or perhaps it was Christchurch, came and bought it without hardly examining it. It was such a good bike, he said, he'd been sad to let it go, but he was glad, really glad, that Don Bayliss hadn't bought it, he wouldn't have wanted to think of that, a suicide cycling off on the bike that had given him so much useful service over the years. He probably would have said more, much more, but I got a call from Louise asking me to go the station and I thanked Mr Entwhistle, telling him that he'd been a great help, and took my leave.

Louise was disappointed. I seemed to be revisiting dead-ends. Why was I talking to Gregory the death-aura hairdresser or Mandy Roberts with her sex-pest story or Mr Entwhistle who couldn't remember anything? Dwight Fricker was meant to be the focus. I'd talked to him. I'd got nothing out of him. Job done. The police position should be clear: the Dwight Fricker angle had been checked out, found to be irrelevant and could be dismissed. She'd like me to tell Mrs Bayliss, as soon as possible, that after careful consideration nothing altered the findings of the original investigation.

I said that my report in that case would be sadly incomplete. She didn't mind.

But, I said, the report would necessarily include my new discoveries, which would only prompt further questions, or perhaps, I added, criticisms.

She looked at me sourly.

I mentioned some of the unfortunate oversights made by the original investigation: the fact that Don was being investigated for embezzlement; that he hadn't been visiting his Alexander Technique teacher on those trips to London; that someone, as yet unknown, had been paying Don a salary for several months leading up to his death. Any one of them might be embarrassing; together, they could prove awkward to explain to senior management. I'd worked on several cases, I said, where the emphasis on past oversights had prompted internal inquiries into the original investigation, which naturally created a whole extra level of work and inevitably put pressure on the original team, some of whom had ended up by being censured.

Louise herself had led the original team.

In any case, I pointed out, Mrs Bayliss would have access to the report, and she would undoubtedly insist, with the forcefulness of her personality and the authority of her position, that any unanswered questions were addressed.

Louise looked at me harshly. 'This better be worth it,' she said.

I called Sylvia to say that I'd like to meet again and she kindly rescheduled a council meeting to fit me in. Sunrise was picture-perfect in the morning sun. It exuded a hush, I felt it enveloping me warmly as I walked up the driveway between the dwarf palms to the front door.

In the beautiful living room we sat, as before, on the enormous sofas. She was wearing a mauve business suit in readiness for her meeting later. I promised her that I only needed a few minutes of her time. I wanted to know if Don had always intended to be an accountant. This was not a question she expected and she peered at me dubiously as if it were a trick. I began to rephrase it and she interrupted. No, she said, when they met, Don had been a little unfocused in his life, unsure what to do. Vaguely, he'd been thinking of publishing, but on reflection, and after they discussed it, publishing seemed too flaky, frankly too unremunerative; finance seemed the better option. He'd always had a good head for numbers.

'A good decision,' she said. 'Don wasn't at first enthusiastic but he agreed.'

I asked her then when they had decided to get married and this time she gave me a frankly critical look. She and Don had been in their mid twenties, she said, they both felt the time was right to settle down, to establish themselves, they came to an understanding very quickly, and after a brief engagement, were married at All Saints Church on Western Avenue, a lovely location in the woods at the head of Branksome Chine, secluded and romantic, where Sylvia had always wanted her wedding, followed by a reception at the Haven Hotel, long a favourite place of hers.

I could tell she was puzzled by these questions and I apologised. It was an unfortunate fact, I said, that the most personal details sometimes prove to be the most important. As it happened, she replied, there wasn't anything particularly personal to say. She'd been attracted to Don partly, or perhaps not so much, for romantic reasons, and partly because she felt, as he did, that they would be good life partners. Don agreed. And so, she said, it turned out.

I waited then. She had begun to reflect and soon she continued. In some ways, she went on, she and Don were opposites. He'd been rather lost when she met him, aimless really. She was the organised one. She was also outgoing, an extrovert. He was quiet, a rather poor talker. Dependable, though, she said, likeable. Everyone liked him. She didn't, at first, think of him as vulnerable. Capable, rather, in an understated way. She herself had always been active, inclined to bursts of energy, sudden changes of direction, she liked to lead. Don, lacking initiative, was the steady one.

'We were married for twenty-six years,' she added.

A long time, I said.

A long time, she repeated. She sighed. And of course over all that time circumstances changed, they changed themselves, she inherited, for instance, they came to live at Sunrise, she became a councillor. Other changes too, she said. But they had always been a good team.

I asked when she had begun to think of Don as 'vulnerable'.

She gave me a sharp look: I was pushing her to the edge of what her habitual briskness could deal with. But she was a strong woman, as I knew, and determinedly honest; soon she went on again. Her miscarriage, she said, had been the first trauma she and Don faced together. But Don couldn't deal with it. At the critical moment, he withdrew, he shrank into himself and left her to face it alone. He hadn't wanted to be a father in the first place, now he didn't want to discuss what to do. This withdrawal, the reluctance to share her pain or to support her through difficult decisions about their future – they even had arguments – had been upsetting at the time, she couldn't deny it. His behaviour looked like selfishness, the half-fearful, half-grudging inaction of the introvert. But later she had come to think of it as weakness, an inability to deal with certain things. After that time, Don went into his shell, became, perhaps, a little peculiar, as closed-up people tend to be. 'He became vulnerable,' she said. 'Needy.'

I thanked her and rose to go. It was in any case time for Sylvia to go to her meeting. But there was an interruption. As we made our way out, there was a knock at the door and when Sylvia opened it, she found a tanned, white-haired man standing there, smiling and gesturing with his hand, in which he carried a jar of home-made preserve. He began to speak but Sylvia cut him off, telling him she was at that moment preparing to leave the house and saying goodbye to me at the same time. So it was that I found myself standing alone on the drive with Ronald Phipps, her next-door neighbour.

He wore raspberry-coloured corduroy trousers and mustard jacket over a sky-blue shirt, and looked like a stereotype of a retired colonel. He wasn't a colonel, however, as he told me immediately, he'd been a banker in Hong Kong, had retired in his early forties and had spent the last thirty years, as he put it, 'perfecting the art of idleness'. His new-looking teeth were very large in his mouth and when he talked he seemed to have difficulty controlling them.

He was keen to chat. He'd been good friends with Sylvia and Don for donkey's years, he said, when I asked. Yes, he said, he'd be happy to answer some questions, delighted in fact to have some company.

His house was on a similar scale to the Bayliss mansion. Appropriately, for a man from Hong Kong, it had a colonial air, with verandas and balconies, and a long, sprawling bungalow shape. We sat on the veranda at the back with our coffees, looking down a lawn smooth and green as baize. Ronald had an erratic manner of talking, fruity tight-lipped ruminations punctuated by short, humorous barks, perhaps a technique developed to prevent his teeth from working their way out of his mouth.

I asked him what he'd thought of Don Bayliss.

'Good chap, no question. Thoroughly decent sort. Liked him, liked him a lot. Didn't say much, but when he got going you knew it was worth saying.'

Could he give me any examples, I asked.

He couldn't. He waved a hand, smiled. 'Water under the bridge. Long time ago, ten years is it, twenty?'

I asked him if he'd found Don boring at all.

'Pretty boring, yes. Thing is, didn't share the same interests. Bored him too, I bet, I tend to bore people. See it in their eyes.'

90

I pointed out that they'd both worked in finance.

Although that was true, Don had been a 'numbers man', Ronald said. Ronald, on the other hand, had worked with clients, in other words the more creative, entrepreneurial side of things. 'Accountants all very well in their place, of course, goes without saying, someone has to keep things tidy, but no excitement in accountancy.' Personally, he liked a bit of excitement, he said. Risk. He'd rarely talked to Don about financial matters.

I asked him what he did talk to Don about.

He couldn't remember.

'Of course,' he said, 'most of the time Sylvia was with us. Lovely woman, well, you've seen her. Very fine woman. But, talk, my word. She was born talking, that woman. Not much chance for anyone else. I often wondered,' he said thoughtfully, 'if, over the years, she'd actually made Don a little deaf. Sometimes, when she was saying something, he'd have this look on his face, as if he literally couldn't hear her. Deaf, I thought, she's damaged his eardrums. On his own, though, his hearing was all right.'

I asked if he remembered any particular occasions when he was on his own with Don.

Yes, he did. They'd occasionally played snooker together. Ronald had a games room, his favourite room. Don had liked it too, admired the paintings he had in there, sports things, cricket, horses and so on. 'He was good at snooker,' Ronald said. 'Surprisingly good. Never got a game off him. Darts the same. Peculiar.' He'd once asked Don how come he was so good, and Don had hummed and hawed and eventually mumbled something about spending most of his youth in snooker halls and pubs.

'Didn't like to talk about it. Before he met Sylvia, see? All that stopped soon as they got together. She didn't like to be reminded of it.'

I told him that Don hadn't originally wanted to be an accountant but he couldn't imagine Don as anything but. 'Numbers man. Not much of a people person. On the spectrum, probably, a lot are. No imagination. I liked him. He could be boring, though, can't deny it.'

Without warning he began to tell me an anecdote. Ronald's house had been broken into, the police couldn't work out how the intruder had got in. 'Don came along, looked round, spotted the problem. Sliding patio doors, insecure. No anti-lift device or some such. Fault in the locking mechanism, something like that.' Don had showed Ronald the doors, explained how they worked, how they ought to work. 'Explained it all in detail, went through it slowly, two or three times, dictation speed. My God. Took forever. Definitely on the spectrum. Anyway, turned out Don used to have the same patio doors, had exactly the same problem, that's how he knew all about it, see?' But what had struck Ronald was the painstaking way Don explained it all, bit by bit, almost as if he were talking to a child. 'Very helpful of him, very, can't deny it. But, well. Hour of my life I wasn't getting back. He could do detail, old Don, but he couldn't do people.'

We finished our coffees and Ronald said he supposed I didn't fancy a bit of a snifter, did I, and I thanked him and said I didn't, and asked him about the break-in.

'What break-in?'

I reminded him what he'd just told me.

Ah yes, he said, that's right, the break-in. The house had been broken into one night while they were all asleep, the intruder came in through the faulty patio doors. At the time they didn't have an alarm.

I asked if anything had been stolen.

Nothing, Ronald said. It had just been unnerving, waking up next morning, realising someone had been in the house. Muddy footprints on the stairs carpet, kitchen cupboards left open. Glass of water on the kitchen table as if the intruder had been thirsty. Ronald's son and daughter-in-law and granddaughter had been staying with them, and that was the frightening thing, to think that someone had been prowling round while the family was there. But nothing was stolen. Ronald's late wife remembered using the en suite at about three in the morning, and the police thought the intruder must have been scared off by the noise.

'Didn't used to be any burglaries round here. Then they started. Quite a few at that time. Bad people, dissolute people, people with no work ethic. Drugs.' He looked at me. 'Sure you don't fancy a snifter? Not long till lunch.' It was a little before eleven.

I asked him when the break-in had been and he laboriously worked it out. 2004, he said with the definiteness of someone who isn't sure.

I thanked him again for his time. As we walked together back to the front of the house, I asked if he thought Don had been happy in his marriage.

'Rum question.' Ronald looked at me but I gave him no guidance. 'None happier,' he said after a moment. 'Don didn't listen and she didn't require any answers.' His teeth clacked in his mouth as he laughed.

What about at the end, after the crash?

Well, the crash had been bad, of course. But a lot of it had been exaggerated by the media, as usual. Personally, Ronald blamed the government, bloody socialists haven't a clue about finance. Anyway, Don was an accountant so he wouldn't have been in the firing line. The investors, the wealth management wallahs, they were the ones took the hit.

So he didn't think Don took his own life because of the crash?

He hummed a bit. Frankly, he wasn't even sure Don killed himself. Most things are accidents, he said. The thing about Don, he said, is he was a private person, he didn't say much and when he did it was tedious stuff like the waffle about the patio doors, you couldn't see into his mind, and even if you could, what you'd see would be nothing but details, numbers, not feelings, like most people.

'Accountants make mistakes,' he said. 'They don't mean to but they do.'

As he shook my hand I could tell that he was itching to ask me again if I fancied a snifter, but he resisted the impulse, and instead told me to come back later if I fancied it; and I said unfortunately I had to go down to the harbour to meet an ex-soldier, and I wouldn't be in Bournemouth very long after that, and he laughed and raised both hands in farewell and stood there watching me go, smart and toy-like in his colourful clothes, a cartoon of the English upper middle classes, a clubbable, friendly man.

My taxi let me out by the Sandbanks Hotel and I went along the harbour road as far as the yacht club, then cut through the car park to the beach and walked the rest of the way on the sand. I was thinking about Don asking

Mr Entwhistle if his bike had lights. It was after Don was told it didn't that he left. Had he been thinking of cycling somewhere at night? I thought of that long, unlit lane out to Hamworthy, when the marina would be deserted and all in darkness. But of course Don's clothes were found not at Hamworthy but at the Haven Hotel. That's where I was heading now, to meet Tom Pollock, the fisherman who'd seen Don sitting on the rocks on the night of 30 October.

It was a bright, warm day, the beach was busy with families, their noises mingling with the noises of the sea, the cries of children with the chattering of marauding herring gulls, the shush and hiss of falling waves. Dogs were permitted here at this time of year; they barked at each other or stood at the water's edge, intent on the oddity of the sea, or capered across the sand, snouts up, pelts ragged in the breeze. One was a cairn terrier and looked so like our old dog Pip that I had to fight the memory. I plodded through the sand. The glittering sea stretched away through the haze to the faint charcoal line of the horizon. Ahead of me was the long, low whale-back of Nine Barrow Down on the other side of the harbour, and I went slowly towards it and came at last to the Haven Hotel.

The hotel stands at the mouth of the harbour, a large, whitewashed building looking down, as if snootily, on the sea agitating uselessly below against a mass of boulders, where fishermen like to sit. For walkers heading for the ferry, there is a narrow concrete walkway between these boulders and the wall of the hotel's patio, and it was on the top of this wall, which is about three metres high, that the bag containing Don Bayliss's clothes and shoes had been found. From the position of the bag it was assumed that Don had thrown it up from the walkway; and the man who claimed he had seen him that night was waiting for me there with his dog.

Like Mr Entwhistle, Tom Pollock had not been believed by the original investigating team. He'd been twenty-five years old then, recently discharged from the army, unemployed and helping the police with their inquiries into a disturbance in a Bournemouth nightclub. His testimony was confused and he'd been mainly anxious to know if there was a reward for his information. Unfortunately, he had to admit consuming five cans of Carlsberg Special Brew during the night in question; his memory of his encounter with 'Don' was inexact and incomplete. Now Tom was a bony forty year old with cropped grey hair and sunken eyes. His many piercings – through his ear, nose, cheek, eyebrow and lower lip – gave intensity to his expression. Something had happened to his teeth: they were unnaturally grey. The tattoo round his throat was grey too. His dog, one of those wiry, whipped-looking mongrels all snout and eyes, exhibited the same nervous energy. While we talked, it kept making quick, creeping dashes along the walkway, and Tom would yell its name, which I never quite caught, and it would come running back in the same way, low to the ground, and wait a moment quivering by Tom's legs, peering round tensely, before dashing off again.

He didn't fish much anymore, Tom said. Too expensive. He was an 'odd-jobber' but work was scarce. He wanted paying for his time but I explained that this would make anything he said unusable in court and he glared at me and looked away but did not leave. He would answer my questions, though first he wanted me to know how hard it was. He was sleeping in a hostel. No one would give him a chance, he said. He had no family. He pulled open his shirt and showed me an army tattoo across his chest. First Battalion Rifles. Only family he'd ever had. Did I know what it meant for people to die for you, actually die? Since his discharge no one was interested in him. He'd take his chances, always had, but he had difficulties, problems with basic understanding, sometimes as if, he said, he had no mental grip at all. In general, things slid away from him, had done all his life. He said all this with bitter anger directed not at me but, it seemed, at the world in general, and I did not feel he was unjustified. Still, he concluded, he wanted to do the right thing now. It was important to him. It was his good name that was at stake, after all.

I asked him about that night. He'd been over there, on that rock (he pointed), fishing. He'd needed to get away, on his own, there was too much going on in his life at that time, it was doing his head in. He sat there all night.

'Not saying I didn't take drink,' he said. 'Not really fishing, to be fair.' It was quiet. Usually there were one or two night fishermen at the same spot, but it was a cool night constantly threatening rain, and he was the only one there, just sitting, sipping from his can, listening to the slap of the waves against the boulders and the occasional screaming fits of the gulls. And at some point he'd looked along the line there and seen in a dim light from a hotel window the man sat on that boulder at the corner, where the path goes round to the car park. Not a fisherman, no rod, net, nothing like that. Just sitting there smoking and staring out to sea. Really no more than a silhouette and the glowing tip of a cigarette. And when Tom had looked again the man had gone.

I asked the obvious questions but Tom had no impression of what he'd looked like, what he was wearing, what he had with him, how long he was there. He couldn't remember if he had a bag with him, he hadn't seen him throw anything on to the hotel wall, he hadn't seen him take off his clothes and go into the sea.

'Did he cough at all?'

'Oh yeah, good point. Like he was trying to bring his guts up. Why I looked across in the first place.'

I said Tom hadn't mentioned any coughing in his original testimony and he shrugged. If no one had asked him about it, it probably wouldn't have come into his mind.

I asked if there was any sign of a bicycle.

There wouldn't be, Tom said. If he'd come on a bike he'd probably have left it in the car park round the corner, by the ferry. He gestured beyond the rock where Don had been sitting.

I asked him if he remembered what time had he seen the man. In the original report, he'd said he had no idea, and it was not thought important enough to follow up, no doubt because if Don had drowned himself that night it mattered little what time it had been exactly. But I did not take that view.

Tom glared at me, said nothing, shook his head, leaned sideways and spat into the water. He felt the injustice of not being able to remember things. His dog ran off, and after a moment he screamed its name and it came back again, looking urgent. Tom had nothing more to say, he'd told me everything. I said I didn't have any more questions anyway, and he relaxed. I asked him what the fishing was like at the harbour and he relaxed a bit more. Four tides every twelve hours, he said. Lots of movement. Bass all year round, mostly school. Come September, good-sized flounder, lots of big mullet, plenty of smooth-hound.

Eels?

'Further along Sandbanks. Sand eels. Conger if you're lucky.'

What about commercial fishing?

'Cod out by Old Harry. Herring turn up Septemberish.' He waved a hand seaward.

Boats out at night?

'Not the trawlers, they're early morning. Lobstermen, though. They go out late, pull in their catch, get back a couple of hours after dark.'

'See any of them that night?'

He thought about that. Just the one, he said, mad old fuck, he'd seen him before but didn't know his name. He came in, driving sloppy, no lights, Tom thought he was going to foul his lines, he'd had to shout at him to keep him off.

I wondered if that was before or after the coughing man was there.

'Oh, he'd gone by then,' Tom said.

His dog returned to base and this time Tom collared him. He had to go to meet someone. I told him I'd put in my report that he'd been very helpful and he gave me a long, suspicious look.

'Do the right thing,' he said, though I couldn't tell whether he was talking about himself or me. I told him again that I couldn't pay but as it happened I had some tickets for private fishing off Bournemouth Pier which, coincidentally, I didn't need, and wondered if he could make use of them. He took the tickets quickly as if afraid I might change my mind, and I watched him go along the walkway, shouting every few moments at his dog, until he disappeared round the corner of the hotel. There are many sorts of missing persons, of course, not only those reported to the police. I went over to the rock at the corner, where he thought he'd seen Don. It was one of a number of boulders dumped there into the sea, which thrashed and churned below. There was no easy route down into the water; in the dark, it would have been almost impossible. Behind me, above the wall, was the hotel bar and terrace. Just round the corner was the ferry. For a prospective suicide it seemed an unlikely spot. I went further along the walkway to an iron ladder and climbed it and found myself in the small car park by the ferry, with a row of benches and a kiosk selling tickets. There was a bicycle rack there too, and I stood for a while, thinking. I had a feeling that if Don Bayliss had killed himself it had not been here but somewhere else. Why come here then? Could it be simply a stopping point for him, a rest on his journey? I tried to see him in my mind, sitting down there on the rocks, smoking a cigarette in the darkness, looking out to sea. It was a charged image. Twenty-six years earlier he had celebrated his wedding at the hotel just behind him; now he squatted in its shadow, performing a tiny act of defiance in smoking a cigarette, which his wife had recently forbidden. Was it an act of repudiation, or of remembrance, or perhaps, more simply, a gesture of farewell? A cigarette or two here, then slipping back up the iron ladder to the car park to retrieve his bike and pedal off . . . somewhere?

As I stood there, I received a text from Sylvia. She wanted to see me. There was something she had forgotten to tell me.

Her council meeting was over but she was still wearing her mauve business suit. As we sat in the living room, Desmond, her husband, appeared and I had my first proper look at him, a tall, stooped man waveringly thin with a look of uncertainty or perhaps innocence on his face. Sylvia quickly dismissed him as she had done before and he at once retreated meekly to another part of the house. Then she handed me a piece of paper. Previously, as requested, she had passed me details of Don's various routines in October 2008, but, she told me now, she had forgotten one of them, a water-sports group of younger people with mental health issues, for which, one evening a week, Don had acted as health and safety advisor. On the paper were details of the group, names of the other organisers and a list of participants. It had been put together with Sylvia's customary efficiency, and I thanked her and asked her if she knew where the group had met.

'Hamworthy marina,' she said.

There was clearly something else on her mind, and almost immediately she began to talk about the upsetting historic allegations of embezzlement made against Don by Marshall Worth. She wanted to know if I could provide any further clarification. She had already, she said, instructed her solicitor to issue Marshall Worth with a demand for an immediate release of all relevant internal documents. I knew this, in fact: Jack Polizzotti had sent me a disgruntled message about it while I was at the Haven. But Marshall Worth were not being helpful, Sylvia said, was there anything I could do? She wanted action. I said there was a man in the Manhattan office, whose name I had been given, and that I would try to get more information out of him, and she was pleased with that and thanked me, and rose to see me out.

At the door, I took the opportunity to ask her about her faulty patio doors, and she looked at me blankly.

I said that, as I understood it from her neighbour Ronald,

they had once, several years earlier, needed to replace their patio doors because of a faulty locking mechanism.

Ronald was wrong, she said. They'd never, at any point, had faulty patio doors. She was very firm about it and I believed her. She was not the sort of woman to make such a mistake. Ronald, she added, was a bit of an imbecile.

It was a soft, warm late afternoon and I took my time walking back to the Ventry Arms. On the way I called Louise and asked for a list of all break-ins in the Branksome Park and Westbourne areas between 2003 and 2008. Then I went on through the leafy, sun-splashed avenues, peering through the foliage at the hidden mansions, telling myself that the same streets had been walked by Robert Louis Stevenson or at least by his disreputable wife.

There had been a change in the guests at the inn, some familiar faces were no longer there, new ones had arrived. The dining room was full again in the evening. There was no sign of Mac. I sat in the window and had the fish pie and crème brûlée, then sat reading *Jekyll and Hyde*. The pace of the story startled me, I'd forgotten how rapidly it moves, with an almost savage speed: in the time it took me to drink my coffee, Sir Danvers Carew had been murdered and Hyde fled, Jekyll had promised Utterson he will never return, and their friend Dr Lanyon, sinking into a fatal illness, had left a sealed letter not to be opened till Jekyll's 'death or disappearance'. I was interested in the sealed letter. There was in the book – as generally in life – an instinctive reluctance to know the worst. Utterson, Lanyon, Enfield all go out of their way to avoid discovering the awful truth, and when they do discover it they immediately take steps to hinder others from discovering it too. Knowing that the sealed letter contains Jekyll's appalling secret, whatever it is, Utterson at once locks it unread in his safe.

Utterson, our reluctant detective, was an interesting character, taciturn, tedious, a stickler for correct behaviour, unwilling to impose himself on others. Was he a little like Don Bayliss? Utterson would also have noticed the faulty locking mechanism of Ronald's patio doors, and explained it all to him in dry detail – but I didn't think he would also have lied about having the same faulty patio doors himself; that was the sign of a different sort of character, a more secretive and more devious one.

The dining room was loud. After my coffee, wanting to continue reading but not wanting to go up to my room so early, I made my way to a small lounge at the back of the inn, where I thought I wouldn't be disturbed, but when I went through the door I found Mac contorted on the carpet in her leotard conducting an online yoga class via her laptop. Though I began to back away again, she beckoned me in. She was just finishing, she said.

In her position I would have been embarrassed, but she wasn't. She explained that the Wi-Fi in her room was patchy and the inn had suggested she use the lounge. They'd said they would put up a *Do Not Disturb* sign on the door, though they had clearly forgotten.

She was flushed and bright-eyed after the exercise, and she stood by the fireplace, breathing hard, her long body taut in high-sheen Lycra. Seeing my copy of *Jekyll and Hyde*, she commented on it, and, as before, we began to discuss it. She wanted to see one of the pictures again, the one of Hyde engulfed in Jekyll's overlarge overcoat standing in front of full-length mirror, and I found the place in the book. Hyde's face isn't visible. But the effect was still disturbing, perhaps more disturbing, without it. Mirrors are such frightening things, Mac said, sources of terror really, perhaps we all have a subconscious fear of them, even as we are drawn to them. The terror of seeing ourselves as others see us, she said, is the worst sort of fear.

Or was it simply the terror of the self, I said? When we look into a mirror, do we think about what we know is hidden, invisibly, inside us, our instincts and secret thoughts? Our desires?

She looked at me for a while, then turned half smiling

to the window, and I gazed at her profile, that nose, her half-smiling mouth, until she turned back to me.

'Are all your secrets painful? Don't you have joy inside you too?'

'Sometimes,' I said, 'to reveal something is to make it disappear.'

'Or to see it for what it really is,' she replied.

There was a short silence. I asked her if she'd read *Mrs Dalloway*. If she was surprised by the change of subject, she didn't show it. She had of course read it; in fact, she'd visited Rodmell in Sussex, where Virginia Woolf had a house and where, in a nearby river, she eventually drowned herself. I asked Mac what she thought of Septimus's suicide, and she said promptly she didn't believe in it. Too obvious, she said. A clumsy set-up. She didn't believe people who actually kill themselves are as fated to do so as he seemed to be. In her opinion, Virginia Woolf herself was very different, perfectly happy for long periods, and her decision to kill herself was a violent, aberrant impulse, the fear of a moment, something to be regretted, if dead people could regret things. If only she'd resisted the impulse, Mac said, she might have been happy for the rest of her life.

'But perhaps that's just my own personality coming out,' she said. 'What do *you* think?'

I said I didn't know.

'Perhaps that's *your* personality coming out,' she said. She smiled at me and lifted her arms in a graceful gesture I could not interpret; then she got up and, reminding me that she wanted us to go together to see the site of Stevenson's house, she left. And after a moment I decided I didn't want to read any more that evening and went up to my room.

'The young man had killed himself; but she did not pity him.' It was the bit about pity that Don had underlined in *Mrs Dalloway*, not the bit about killing himself. The previous pages in the novel make it clear that Mrs Dalloway regards Septimus's suicide positively, as an act of 'defiance' in the face of 'intolerable life', a means of bravely preserving the precious thing inside him – whatever that was – before it can be corrupted. I thought of Don Bayliss, a man of secrets, who hid whatever was inside *him*. Had *he* killed himself to preserve something precious before it disappeared?

I read through the paper Sylvia had given me, the details of the youth water-sports group, the names of leaders and participants. Several shared a surname; I had the impression of local families, siblings and parents. These were the people Don Bayliss had seen each week. I opened the window to the night and let in the scent of pine and lay down on my bed again. Were all my own secrets painful, as

Mac had asked? I thought of my family and, as before, on the beach, a memory of our old cairn terrier Pip came to me; I seemed to see him strutting on the sand, and before I could stop it, a memory followed of my eleven-year-old son Sami cavorting alongside him. It was somewhere in France, La Rochelle perhaps, where we used to go on holiday. I saw our apartment in Paris too, the stairs up to it, the apartment door wide open, the kitchen floor, the refrigerator in the corner, and Maria at the sink turning towards me, her face still tanned from the holiday sun, smiling. And then, as always, I saw the road to Chartres ahead of us, bright as metal, sunlight smashing off it, and the truck suddenly appearing in front of us, big and dark as a falling cliff, blocking everything out. This is not an original memory; in fact, I remember nothing of the accident, it is a reconstruction, what I was told much later, when they explained to me what had happened and how my wife and son were killed, it is a memory my brain has supplied because it seems that to have nothing would be worse.

I lay unmoving on my bed. Sometimes there is nothing to be done with memories but endure them until they release the body.

Unfortunately, when the images fade from my mind there is no relief, for what always happens then is the renewal of my sense of loss, of permanent, irrevocable loss, for though

I am a finder I will not find my family, they are not missing, they are not coming back.

My phone rang and I found myself standing at the window, now closed, gazing at my own reflection in the pane. It was eleven o'clock.

Louise said, 'You need to get yourself to London . . . Yes, now.'

I read through the report in the taxi. The Metropolitan Police had arrested a man called Michael McCullers, known as 'Mario', on suspicion of murder and were holding him at Lewisham Station. He was a white man, thirty-six years old, with a long history of convictions including counterfeiting, robbery and, more recently, the abduction and rape of a minor. The previous night, the body of his sixteen-year-old pregnant girlfriend had been found at the bottom of a stairwell in a high-rise at Loampit Vale. Mario had been threatening her and several witnesses had seen him arguing violently with her a few hours before her body was discovered. None of this seemed relevant to me. But when the officers were booking Mario in at Lewisham they discovered he was wearing a wristwatch with the name *Donald Bayliss* inscribed on the back.

I read the report carefully, made a couple of calls to all-night departments at places where I used to work, and by the time we reached Lewisham High Street, shortly before two o'clock, had a little extra information, including Mario's employment records. At the station they were expecting me, and I was taken straight through to the custody suites and into a consultation room, one of the little booths used mainly for solicitor visits, where I waited for Mario to be brought from the cells. They'd warned me that he might not be cooperative but he came in a few moments later without any bother and sat down opposite me. He had a bad limp and looked tired, his face stubbled and slack, shadows under his eyes, though it was still a handsome face; he was one of those ageing young men, mildly debauched, with prominent cheekbones and longish dyed-dark hair falling in an arc across his forehead, wearing a battered but still spectacular blue pinstripe jacket with wide lapels and primrose-yellow cravat. He had an almost amiable sneer, as if the world had become ridiculous to him, and a picturesque habit of sweeping the hair back from his forehead with a casual hand. He called me 'man'. I thought he was being careful not to act like someone about to be charged with murder. The idea of a link between him and Don seemed ridiculous.

I asked him if he wanted anything. He wanted to know the time, he said. They'd taken away his watch. I said that apparently the watch had once belonged to Donald Bayliss and asked him how he'd come by it, and he repeated what he'd said to the officers already, that he really couldn't remember. He had plenty of friends in the pre-owned jewellery trade, he said, he owned a lot of 'quality gear' picked up on the cheap that way, and probably he'd got this watch from one of them. I dropped the subject then and asked him about himself generally. Wanting distraction, he was willing to speak. It was obvious, in fact, he was the sort of man eager to talk about himself. Music had been one of his great and motivating passions, he said, he'd once been a member of a promising band that toured Europe but never quite made it; since it broke up, he'd been involved on the fringes of the industry, sometimes as a manager or advisor, running tickets or managing clubs and other performance venues, occasionally, he admitted, as supplier of high-end recreational drugs to the stars, some of whom had become his 'bros'. He dropped some names, offhandedly mentioned famous gigs in Buenos Aires, Tokyo, Reykjavik. It was clear that what he really liked about music was the lifestyle, its sleazy glamour, backstage buzz, the berserking of the crowds and the groupies waiting in the back streets when the crowds are gone. The groupies in particular he liked, and young groupies most of all. Mario had a record of relationships with underage girls, one of which had ended in the conviction for abduction and rape.

I watched him as he told me these things. Slouching on his chair, he talked slowly, almost drawling, exuding confidence, a sort of cheek, though all the time his thigh was twitching up and down. Once he'd been charming, now he seemed mainly seedy. He had a number of 'pads' in South-East London, where he liked to 'crash', he said, and a place of his own in respectable Camberwell, but essentially, he said, he was a 'rolling stone', living for highs, meaningful experiences – a once-in-a-lifetime set by an unheard-of band, say, a trip of pure chemical excitement, a starry night in a field with a girl who has never been kissed before. He looked at me slyly, tossed away that lock of hair. He liked himself but was aware of his vanity and humbug; his amiable sneer was partly aimed at himself, and in truth I could imagine his success with unwary young women.

After he'd been talking for about twenty minutes I observed that he didn't seem very anxious about a possible murder charge. He gave me that smile again, shrugged. The officer who brought me in said he thought the CPS would struggle to bring a charge unless they could scrape up more evidence. I also observed that Mario didn't seem much bothered by the death of the expectant mother of his child, and his smile disappeared then, he looked away and his leg went up and down a little faster.

Getting out my phone, I scrolled through his employment records. As he'd said, he'd worked at quite a few venues over the years. Most of these, I observed to him, were actually table-dancing bars and strip clubs, where the music was incidental. He became defensive. Usually, he'd been managing them on a temporary basis, occasionally, he admitted, filling in for bar staff. His life began to sound a lot less glamorous. Of course, he organised the acts too, he said. I mentioned two or three of the clubs. Hot and Wet. Bacchus. Kink. He acknowledged them. I pointed out that they were owned by Dwight Fricker. He didn't hesitate or equivocate. Yeah, he knew Dwight, he'd worked with Dwight directly on one or two big events.

I asked him about Dwight.

He thought Dwight knew what he was doing, business-wise, and was generally sensible, though liable to run amok, as was well known. But they got on. They were tight, in fact, looked out for each other. He'd visited him in prison. 'Did you know he paints? Fucking awful things.'

There was one of Dwight's clubs I was particularly interested in, I said. Taboo. Mario had worked there for a couple of months, September and October 2008.

'That's right,' he said.

Is that where he'd met Don Bayliss?

He started to nod and caught himself too late. He gave out a sort of chuckle. 'Like one of them telephone salesmen, aren't you? Lots of little questions don't mean nothing, then you suddenly realise you've gone and bought something.' He shrugged, wiped that lock of hair off his forehead. He was too lazy to lie anymore. 'All right. Don was one of the punters, yeah.'

He had nothing to hide and was happy to tell me what I wanted to know. Don had been a regular visitor to Taboo while Mario had been there. Nice guy, Mario said, harmless, not like some of them, guys who shout and get messy, guys who want the girls hog-tied or flamed. Just a regular fellow enjoying the shows, buying the girls drinks, letting his hair down, getting a little something he didn't get at home. A type very common at such clubs, overweight, balding execs still wearing their business suits with just enough physical energy to play out a last few fantasies.

'Most of them just watch,' Mario said.

Was Don just a watcher?

Don liked a little action too, but a lot of the time he sat at the bar and talked; that's how Mario had got to know him. He'd been in a bad way, health-wise, if he remembered. Hacking cough.

I asked what Don had talked about and Mario gave me

a brief but accurate account of Don's home life, the sort of house he lived in, the sort of wife he had, and the job he did. Don had told him all these things.

I asked if Mario had ever given Don one of Dwight Fricker's cards.

He thought about it. Yes, actually, he remembered doing that.

But why? He thought about it a bit more. Dwight was looking for accountancy support, someone kosher, so when Mario found out Don worked in finance he gave him the card, though he had no idea whether Don had followed up on it. He'd formed the impression Don was fundamentally timid, as most punters are, even – or especially – the drunks, a little wild when they're safely inside with the girls, but taking great care no one recognises them coming in or going out.

I asked him then how he ended up with Don's watch.

Don gave it to him, he said at once. Don didn't explain the gift, just said something vague about not needing it anymore. The giving of it didn't seem out of character; Don was a friendly guy, after all, and obviously well off, and Mario had made his visits to the club nice and comfortable. They'd shared time. But after Don's death, which he'd been shocked to read about, it made a different sort of sense, it seemed then like a farewell gesture, a divestment, and Mario had kept it in acknowledgement of the moment, and over time had come to think of it, in some sense, as a significant object passed in ritual from one man to another in his preparations for death. It had spiritual meaning. He hoped the police would give it back to him soon. I paid little attention to this flight of fancy, though it clearly excited Mario. His life, as I say, was made up of these highs. I asked him instead if he thought Don was the type to kill himself. No, he said at once, not at all; although, he added, unable to resist philosophising, it was true that quiet, straightforward people are the likeliest to hide their true selves, he had known many people like that, and indeed, he added, with only the slightest trace of irony, he put himself in that category.

Back in Bournemouth, I slept until noon and woke groggy. I could hear lunchtime noises from the bar and restaurant downstairs, voices, laughter, the clatter of crockery. Sunlight came in round the edges of the curtains, striping the adjacent and opposite walls of my room with bands of glowing orange, and, as if caught in this faintly luminous network, for minutes I lay there, unable to get up, thinking about Don Bayliss. His known movements on the afternoon and evening of his disappearance were at least a little clearer to me. At three thirty, in the East Cliff Café down at the Bournemouth front, he'd encountered Gregory but didn't want to speak to him and, indeed, seemed anxious for him to leave. At five o'clock, he'd visited Mr Entwhistle in Parkstone but didn't buy his bicycle after being told that it had no lights. At some time between six o'clock, when it got dark, and eight o'clock, by which time, according to Tom Pocock, the last of the lobstermen had come back, he'd sat on the rocks under the wall of the hotel where he'd celebrated his wedding twenty-six years earlier, smoking a cigarette. And then finally – I thought – he'd left to go somewhere else. So much was clear to me. But Don himself was even more badly out of focus. He was the stickler for good conduct who was being investigated for embezzlement, the sensitive, considerate manager hitting on a vulnerable young member of staff, and now, thanks to Mario, he was also the dull and dutiful husband visiting strip joints where he could play out his sleazy sexual fantasies, a middle-aged man who 'liked them young'. I thought of Don weeping in the Marshall Worth hospitality suite next to a newspaper carrying the story of a teacher who had run off with his fourteen-year-old student. There were large and alarming disconnections in these images of Don, but I found myself thinking more of the little discrepancies: the man who doesn't read books going through the novels of Virginia Woolf carefully making notes; the man who follows his interminably boring account of some patio doors' faulty locking mechanism with the quite needless lie that he'd owned the same doors himself, as if to explain how he knew they could be opened.

And I thought of Jekyll and Hyde, not their co-existence, but the way one changes violently into the other, and why. And then it was time for my arranged long-distance call with Sol Abramowitz in New York.

Sol's voice was a surprise, not the sort of dry, powerful voice I expected from a corporate finance CEO, but a warm and lively voice inclining to humour. It conjured up a different man from the small, compact one whose face appeared on the company website, someone thick-set, a big, bluff man with body hair, a fondness for a beer and the sort of eyes of overflowing emotion that never leave you. He told me it was good to speak, wanted me to know it was a treat to hear an old-fashioned, snooty Limey accent. He was going to put me on speakerphone, he said, so his assistants could hear too. 'It's all about the accent. I got people gathering here just to get a load of it, there's quite a crowd, I'm gonna start selling nuts.' He told me he was kidding. I hadn't expected the Vice President and Head of Internal Affairs at Marshall Worth Financial Group to be a kidder, either; I was impressed, and told him so, and he laughed for almost half a minute. But he was a fast talker too, and time, of course, was money. Before I could ask any of my questions he started to talk about Don, not at first about his role in the company or the nature of Don's liaison with his American colleagues, but about his person, his personality. Over the years Sol had seen a lot of Don, two or three times a year for approximately ten years. He'd loved him, he said, loved his accent, of course, loved his understatement, dependability, loved even his pedantry. They'd all loved him, everyone in the office, the old guys, the younger folk, the young women, they couldn't get enough of those old-world manners.

'We got on,' Sol said, 'like a house on fire.' He'd never been so sad to lose a colleague, he said, he'd been devastated, they all had, it was a terrible, terrible thing. But now, he said, after time had passed, he treasured the memories. He began to reminisce. There was a weekend he particularly treasured. He'd got Don up to his cabin in Connecticut and they'd fished together, though frankly, he said, Don wasn't much of a fisherman. More of a home bird, he thought, and he loved hearing Don talk about his house, his garden, his wife. 'I guess you Brits just love your home life,' he said. I asked if he'd ever visited Don in the UK, and he said a couple of times, and I wondered if he'd met Sylvia, and he said no, but he knew from Don that she was a queen among women.

After all this free-flowing enthusiasm had run its course, I asked him if he thought Don had been a needy person. At this, he hesitated; his voice lost its cartoon bonhomie. No, he said, more thoughtfully, not exactly needy, professionally never, even emotionally, no, he didn't think so – but on the other hand . . . there was sometimes something *melancholy* about him. At the time it had been easy to take it for the famous British pessimism, but in retrospect he felt it was a part of Don's character.

I asked then about Don's role at Marshall Worth and he gave me a rapid summary. 'Ethical oversight' was one of the specs he listed, and I said that it must have been awkward when Don had faced allegations of personal financial wrongdoing. There was another pause; I wondered if he'd caught what I'd said and had begun to repeat myself when he interrupted me. His voice had changed again, and now it was the dry, powerful one I'd expected at first. He expressed concern that I was in possession of information not meant for external consumption. He would let that ride, though, he said, on the understanding that this was a confidential call and that I was a person of no significance in the financial world, and because he'd liked Don and wanted to make sure the record was straight. But he would be brief, take no questions, and never return to the subject. Without waiting for my response, he described the situation in October 2008 when an apparent error, small but somewhat alarming, had been discovered in the Bournemouth office, leading to unfortunate doubts about the nature of Marshall Worth's global business at a time when the company was in anxious negotiations with the Fed about the need for ongoing support. Though this possible error had grave implications, it wasn't large in itself, so the question was how to contain it in the short term. Don suggested shifting the source of the problem away from wealth and asset management to accountancy, and setting up an investigation into personal wrongdoing, an uncontroversial and relatively common procedure arousing little special interest, which would divert attention from corporate function on to individual agency. For this, Don volunteered himself. It would buy the company time in which to interrogate the nature of the apparent error without the Fed becoming overexcited. Their only real concern then would be to avoid the sort of local staff disquiet that always accompanies such inquiries, so it was decided to run everything from New York and maintain complete radio silence in the UK. In due course they were able to investigate the original error, rectify it (a minor matter, as it turned out), and explain it all, several months later, to the Fed's complete satisfaction. In short, Don was never actually under investigation. His written depositions, the interviews with lawyers, removal of his privileges, suspension of his salary and so on were all part of the charade for the Fed. Marshall Worth continued to pay him, in fact, direct from New York.

'So Don didn't embezzle anything?'

'Of course he didn't.' Sol laughed. 'I can't imagine Don doing anything wrong. He wouldn't even stretch his expenses a little. That was the joke part of it all.'

After that, true to his word, Sol did not allow any questions or comments. He reverted briefly to his warm and humorous voice, though in a distracted way, as if someone else were now in the room and another meeting was beginning. But it didn't matter, I already had what I needed. We ended the call on a note of trivial goodwill, and ten minutes later I left the inn and set out through the pleasant avenues for Sunrise.

Sylvia listened to my version of what Sol Abramowitz had told me. She was relieved, of course, but she'd expected as much, she said. It had been obvious that Don would never have done anything wrong, he simply wasn't that sort of man. Though how typically self-sacrificing, not to say naïve, of him to volunteer for the role of fictional embezzler. She made an impatient noise; she couldn't imagine any of his colleagues stepping up in the same way, exposing themselves to the possibility of the wrong idea getting out.

I asked her if Don used to talk much about his trips to New York. Did he enjoy them, look forward to them? Had they been a welcome break from his regular work in the Bournemouth office? Perhaps he'd told her about the pleasant weekend in Sol's cabin in Connecticut. But she didn't even recognise Sol's name. She said only that Don usually came home from the US complaining that he had even more work to do. He didn't like Americans much, she added.

Given that Don had been in no danger from Marshall Worth's 'investigation', I suggested that the pressure he'd felt at work was perhaps a little less than we'd previously thought. But she was not ready to exonerate the company as easily as that, and made no comment. I wondered out loud if there had been any other source of pressure, and she looked at me expectantly. She could tell I had something else on my mind but was finding it hard to say.

'Have you heard of club called Taboo?' I asked at last.

As I described it, the colour drained from her face until she was grey, a terrible contrast with both her gold hair and her primrose-coloured suit. But, after listening in silence, she said only – in a tightly constrained voice – that the man called Mario must be a fantasist. I replied that unfortunately it seemed to me that Don had indeed visited the club and talked to Mario there. I explained that it was owned by

Dwight Fricker, and that Mario was the one who had given Dwight's card to Don. That made her pause but she didn't like it any better. We were heading for a confrontation so there was nothing to be lost and I asked her then if she might be able to tell me what sexual relations had been like between herself and Don.

For a moment she just stared at me, then, flushing violently, rose from the sofa, as if to escort me off the premises. I stayed where I was and soon she sat down again and brought herself under control. A minute or two passed, very slowly, while she decided what to do. Then she spoke. She had not expected to find herself facing such personal questions but she would give me an answer and then not speak of the subject again. There had been no sexual relations between herself and Don for many years before his disappearance. As she had already told me, they slept in separate bedrooms. After her miscarriage she had suffered gynaecological complications and, after they had been resolved, her body was not as before, nor her attitude. But Don, she added, had never been a sexual person. He was in fact quite frigid and disliked being touched, so the lack of sexual relations did not affect him in any way. The idea that he was driven to find pleasure in a club where women danced naked on tables and performed lewd sex acts in booths was not only offensive but also bizarre. Don was simply not that sort of man. She was surprised, she said, that I had been taken in by this Mario. I thanked her for her candour and apologised for having to ask such questions.

She wanted to ask me a question in return, she said. A blunt one. Was I in fact any nearer to finding out what had happened to Don? I thought about that and said that I had reached the stage when the investigation opens up or closes down, but I could not tell as yet which it would be. She was irritated by this, and I did not blame her, but I could not help it. I thanked her again and left.

Down at the front, at Branksome Chine beach, I sat on one of the benches on the long sweep of esplanade and watched the afternoon light changing the colours of the water. The sand was crowded with families: they lay on towels surrounded by their belongings, or pottered at the edge of the sea, or dug holes with their children. There were many children. I remembered my own childhood in Baghdad, lazing all summer on the roof of our house reading murder mysteries, Inspector Maigret or Hercule Poirot stories, in paperback editions picked up in Paris by my father, greedy not so much for the unwinding plots but for the lives of the people who appeared in them, the secondary characters, the witnesses, charladies, concierges, cab drivers, school teachers, shop assistants, all the teeming crowds of those usually invisible people who stepped forward for a moment and for once spoke for themselves.

I considered once more what Mario had told me. He was a liar, of course, but liars sometimes tell the truth too.

After a while, I read through the report prepared for me by Louise's team on the spate of break-ins in Branksome Park and Westbourne between 2003 and 2008. There were fewer than Ronald Phipps had imagined: half a dozen in all, of which three had never been solved. Two of the unsolved break-ins were straightforward burglaries; it was the other one that caught my attention. In Cassel Avenue, less than a mile from Sunrise, the Forsters' house had been broken into one night in July of 2008. Nothing was taken and it was only in the morning, when the fourteen-year-old daughter, Lucia Forster, said that she had heard someone moving about in the night, that they realised a break-in had taken place. The reason this caught my attention was because I had seen the name Lucia Forster somewhere else. It was on the list of participants in the water-sports group at Hamworthy marina which Don Bayliss attended as health and safety coordinator.

I sent some follow-up questions to Louise, finished my ice cream and made my way through the milling holiday crowds along the esplanade and up The Avenue towards the Ventry Arms.

Before dinner I had time to kill and went out on to the little lawn and sat on a chair under a striped awning to read *Jekyll and Hyde*. The story moved on with the same reckless speed as before, and abruptly arrived at the end, the body of Hyde found on the floor of Jekyll's dissecting room, Jekyll missing, and nothing left to do except read a mysterious letter addressed to Utterson, which will reveal the truth at last. Again, this business of sealed letters! Explanations are provided only after the calamity has taken place, the story understood only after it is finished and cannot be prevented from taking its awful course. We have been helpless, gripped by our atavistic instincts – our revulsion at the 'haunting sense of unexpressed deformity' projected so disturbingly by Hyde, the air of a depravity that cannot be named – but paralysed by incomprehension. Nor do we want to know. On the contrary, we wish to insulate ourselves from knowledge. I thought of Mandy recoiling confused from Don in the little kitchen at Marshall Worth, or Gregory cringing without knowing why at Don's unnatural awkwardness in the East Cliff Café. As I was thinking these things, Mac appeared. She stood against the sunlight dressed as before in a tracksuit and asked if I wanted to go with her to Skerryvore.

On the way we talked about books. Over the years she'd read an enormous number, and I asked her if she'd always been a reader and she said no, it had come on her quite suddenly, out of the blue, when she was sixteen. Before then, she didn't read anything at all. I asked if she remembered what that first book had been and she told me it was John Fowles's *The Magus*, 700 pages of closely typeset text, which she'd read literally non-stop from start to finish. Why had she chosen that book, I asked? It had been the only book in English in the store where she happened to be at the time, she said, and fell silent. Then we arrived at Skerryvore and began to talk, naturally enough, about Stevenson. He lived in the house for only two years, but managed to write both *Kidnapped* and *Jekyll and Hyde* there. Mac knew the house's layout and guided me round the foundations – 'This was the vestibule, this the drawing room, the stables were over there' – talking about the many visits Henry James paid Stevenson during the summer of 1885, when they would have sat together in those rooms, often with Fanny too, talking about writing and their respective work. Mac had a theory. Apparently, at the beginning of the year Stevenson had been working on an adventure story called *The Dynamiters* – just his sort of thing. James was preoccupied with his usual psychological stories. Yet, shortly after

131

these conversations, Stevenson began *Jekyll and Hyde*, much more psychological than anything he'd ever done, and, equally strange, James began to write an adventure story about bomb-throwing anarchists, *The Princess Casamassima*. It was as if they'd swapped interests.

'Or personalities,' she said.

I asked her why she thought they might have done that and she shrugged. Each of them, she said, was already a dual personality in a way – Stevenson the bohemian with the conventional instincts of the upper middle class, James the closet homosexual – each hiding a part of themselves, as many, perhaps most, people do. She mentioned my work. Perhaps it was true, she said, that sometimes a missing person is actually finding another part of themselves, liberating something in themselves that they've been hiding for years.

She'd expressed an interest in missing people before, and I asked her if she herself had known anyone who disappeared. By now we were standing at the end of the garden where the ground falls away steeply into the overgrown chine, and for a moment she didn't reply, looking down into the tangled green shadows, her profile outlined against the afternoon light.

Yes, she said at last. She had known someone.

And were they found?

'Depends what you mean.' Still staring into the chine, she began to tell me the story. Mac had grown up in a small, remote town called Tuatapere situated on a river plain east of the Southern Alps, at the southern tip of New Zealand's South Island. Only about two hundred families lived there. Her best friend was a girl called Fran Malone. Their fathers worked together at one of the sawmills, as most of the local men did. Like many children, Fran was a good runner when she was young. Unlike most others, as she got older she didn't stop being good. She got better. She ran in the hills, along the coast, up the river, she was always running. And when she was eleven, she was spotted by an athletics coach who was hiking in the area. Apparently, Fran's times were better than good, they were freakish. There were discussions with her family, at the end of which Fran went away to a sports-specialist boarding school in Christchurch. She wasn't happy there but she didn't stop running and she didn't stop getting better. She ran the 800 and 1,500 and by the time she was sixteen her personal bests were only a few seconds outside the current world records. She was, as they say, a prodigy. Her races were shown on television, her photograph appeared in newspapers, magazines, she became the running girl from the back of beyond, 'The Quick Hick', and in 2004, still only sixteen years old, she was chosen to represent New Zealand at the Athens Olympics.

Mac said, 'I saw her a few days before she flew off with the rest of the squad. She had half an hour to spare between photo shoots.' For months Fran's smiling face had been everywhere; she was the most talked-about person in the country. Everyone expected her to win golds. Mac glanced at me. 'She'd developed this nervous tic. All the time she talked her eye was jumping.' Then she'd flown off with the other Olympians and shortly after reaching the hotel in Athens she disappeared.

I waited.

Four days later Fran Malone was found alive in a janitor's cupboard in the Baggage Reclaim Area at the airport, where she had been hiding, and was flown home without competing at the games. Her face was still everywhere, only this time it was a hard face, bitter and closed-up, with one drooping eye, appearing under headlines like *Gold Medal Hope Crashes Out Before Starting*.

It was dinner time and we walked back through the garden and along the lovely avenues to the inn.

'What became of her?' I asked.

Mac shrugged. She'd never seen Fran Malone again. But she smiled. 'I'm an optimist, I like to think she found herself in that cupboard.'

She looked at me and I saw how beautiful and also how sad her eyes were.

'Perhaps,' I said, 'she had a copy of *The Magus* to read.'

'Perhaps,' she said, after a moment.

'And grew up an optimist and became a yoga and aerobics teacher.'

Then she laughed, making that sound I'd heard and liked so much before. 'Don't be so pleased with yourself,' she said. 'Don't think I've told that story to anyone who didn't immediately guess who I was talking about.'

We reached the Ventry Arms.

'Dinner?' she said.

But as we walked towards the dining room, I got a message from Louise asking to see me straight away and I made my apologies. Mac reminded me that she was going home in two days' time and I asked if she would have dinner with me the next night.

'Will you have found your person by then?'

I said it was possible. I watched her go into the dining room, then crossed to Reception and asked the lady there to call a taxi for me.

Louise was angry. There had been complaints.

I asked what complaints.

'Where to start?' she said. She started with Marshall

Worth. Divulging confidential information in a manner likely to be prejudicial, according to Jack Polizzotti, who had called Louise to ask that my investigation be halted. I said that I'd now spoken to a more senior, more helpful figure in New York, who'd been willing to corroborate the information, given that I was – to quote him – a person of no significance in the financial world. I gave her Sol Abramowitz's name and suggested she call him. I added that I wouldn't be pursuing that line of inquiry any further.

'What about the widow?' Sylvia had also contacted Louise to tell her how uncomfortable she had been with my new line of questioning, which was in itself borderline impertinent and not only unenlightening but in fact confusing. As it happened, Louise was due to attend the next council meeting and Sylvia had asked if they could meet beforehand to discuss the matter.

I told her about Mario and Taboo, and her professional curiosity got the better of her. She didn't like what I told her, however. She didn't like the complication. Did I think he was telling the truth about Don's watch?

'Up to a point,' I said. She looked at me mistrustfully.

She wanted to know about the Haven Hotel.

I said that if Don had died, it wasn't there. She didn't like this much either.

She wanted to know about the bicycle.

I said that it didn't suit Don's purpose because it didn't have lights.

She didn't like any of it. It wasn't neat, it wasn't timely or cheap. I could tell by the way she looked at me that she held me responsible for these inconveniences.

'Are you telling me he might even be still alive somewhere?' she asked, as if this would be the most untidy, expensive and least satisfactory outcome of all.

I said I didn't know yet, I was only sure he hadn't killed himself.

'Christ,' she said.

I reminded her then about my follow-up questions about the Forster family who had been broken into in Cassel Avenue in 2008 and she handed me the information I'd asked for. I was in luck. The family was still living in the same house.

Louise wanted to know why I was interested in the Branksome and Westbourne break-ins, and I told her that it would be a little clearer once I'd talked to the Forsters, in particular the daughter, Lucia, who'd been fourteen at the time of the break-in. In that case, Louise said, I was actually out of luck: Lucia was no longer alive; tragically, she had taken her own life while still a teenager.

After a moment, I asked her when that had been.

She consulted her records. September 2008, she said. Just a month before Don Bayliss disappeared.

I asked how she had died and Louise told me she had drowned herself at Hamworthy marina.

Like the other houses in the street, the Forsters' was a large detached villa of red brick and stucco, with great bay windows and a red tile roof. I could see immediately why it might have appealed to an intruder: it was flanked at one side by the overflowing garden of its neighbour, through which someone might make their way without much fear of being seen, and the fence between them did not look insurmountable. At the back, overlooking a long, immaculate lawn, a modern conservatory had been added, opening out on to an attractive stone patio. As I sat there with Richard Forster, I asked him if he'd ever had a problem with his patio doors. Richard was sixty years old, an overweight, genial man with a round head largely bald, shabbily dressed in pink shorts and two T-shirts, the outer one of which bore the slogan *Sous les Pavés, la Plage!* He owned an IT consultancy company, he'd told me, though he didn't do much in it anymore. He had a gentle smile.

'Funny you should say that,' he said. The doors we were looking at weren't the original ones. The old ones had been replaced after the break-in of 2008. They had been insecure; a fault in the locking mechanism. The intruder had entered through them. Still, Richard went on, it happened long ago and nothing was taken. Besides, at that time, there had been other things demanding the family's attention. Perhaps, he said, I knew his daughter had taken her own life shortly afterwards. I apologised for raking up the past, and he gave me his smile again, which I saw wasn't gentle at all but quietly agonised, even after so many years.

It had been Lucia, he said, who raised the alarm about the break-in the following morning. At first they hadn't believed her, she was prone to morbid delusions, particularly at night, but when he looked round he discovered that the patio doors were unlocked, though he was sure he'd locked them the previous evening, and that one of the trellis panels bordering their neighbour's garden was broken where it seemed someone had climbed over. Oddly, there was also a glass half full of water left on the kitchen table as if the intruder had poured himself a drink.

I asked what Lucia had reported and he said that she'd

140

woken in the night to hear noises on the landing outside her room and that as she turned towards her half-open bedroom door someone standing out of sight quietly closed it. But, Richard said, Lucia had been very ill at the time, prey to all sorts of fantastical thoughts. I apologised again for reminding him of old traumas. Yes, he said, it had certainly been traumatic. She had been such a happy little girl but somehow when she became a teenager she lost a sense of herself, she didn't seem to know who she was anymore, as if some ordeal emptied her out and left her helpless, prey to any sort of paranoid fantasy. I asked Richard if professionals had been able to identify a cause of Lucia's illness and he said that no such cause had ever been found, though certain factors, such as self-esteem, body image and peer relationships, had clearly all exacerbated her distress. There had never been any involvement with drugs, he added.

I asked him about the community support available to Lucia, and, among other things, Richard mentioned the youth water-sports group that met at Hamworthy, which Lucia had enjoyed, though it had been there that she had drowned, so they found it difficult now to think of the group without pain. I took the opportunity to ask if Richard remembered Don Bayliss, who, I said, was the health-and-safety coordinator for the group. I showed him a picture, and after a moment he said yes, a kindly man, if he was remembering right, very unathletic, but gentle with the kids. I asked if Lucia had liked him, and Richard said she had, yes, it was noticeable that she liked talking to him, they could often be seen on their own together. In general she enjoyed the group sessions, they all did, in fact, they turned them into family trips and went down together and spent the afternoon at the marina.

I returned to the subject of the break-in and asked if Richard could show me where Lucia had heard the intruder. We went up the stairs together. Lucia had said she first heard footsteps outside her room, then going along the landing, and then, a little later, going down the stairs. Finally, she heard the distinctive swishing sound of the patio doors closing. We stood outside Lucia's bedroom: Richard did not offer to show me inside and I did not ask him to let me see it. I asked which rooms were further along the landing.

The bathroom, he said, their bedroom, a third bedroom and, at the end, a box room, where at the time the baby, Lucia's little brother, slept. Unfortunately, Richard said, the arrival of the baby caused difficulties with Lucia, who was often hostile, sometimes developing angry obsessions with the baby's things, clothing for instance or toys, which she would take from the baby's room and claim were really hers. Just after the break-in, if he remembered, she became fixated on a small stuffed rabbit, which she said wasn't the baby's at all, but her own; someone, 'an admirer', had given it specially to her. This was almost certainly not true. Richard remembered the incident because they lost their tempers and fought over it, which of course only made it worse, and Lucia became so agitated that her medication had to be increased. He regretted it now, bitterly. Imagine, he said, fighting over a toy rabbit. It was so trivial. They'd never noticed the stupid thing before, they couldn't even remember buying it for the baby, though they surely must have done, it meant nothing to them, they should just have let Lucia hang on to it. Indeed, he said in anguish, they'd spent the last months of their daughter's life doing nothing but disbelieve her, arguing with her, fighting over trivial things, and now his last memories of her were of desperate and angry confrontations. He wished instead they'd believed everything she told them, all of it, all the nonsense, all the fantasies, gone along with all of them, just so he could remember those months differently now.

By this time, we were back in the conservatory. I asked what had happened to the rabbit and he looked at me oddly. He thought it was still in Lucia's room, and I asked if I could see it. Though he clearly thought this strange, he went upstairs to fetch it for me, and I sat alone wondering why an intruder would go to the very great trouble of breaking in without taking anything.

Richard returned with the toy rabbit. It was light in my hand, small enough for a very young child to hold, fawn-coloured with pink ears, one of those soft animals with child-like features, big head and large innocent eyes. The strange thing, Richard said, was that they never knew where it had come from, it seemed to be second-hand, though they'd rarely bought second-hand things.

I turned it over. There was a name neatly handwritten in ink on the label underneath.

Adrian Bayliss.

Back at the Ventry Arms I went up to my room and lay on my bed. Had Don broken into the Forsters' house in order to leave behind one of the toys bought for his own stillborn son? It was bizarre – though, I supposed, no more bizarre than calmly walking out of a business meeting one afternoon and disappearing. And I saw now that there were things I'd got backwards.

After a while I got off the bed and got busy. I called Louise's office to get details for Mr Entwhistle's daughter. I wanted to find out the name of the website on which her father had advertised his bicycle. Then I took a taxi into Bournemouth, to the offices of the company, where I was given a place to perch while I logged onto their system and accessed their archive for October and November 2008. By lunchtime I had the names and addresses of two people in the Bournemouth and Poole areas who, coincidentally, had also been advertising second-hand bicycles for sale on the website at the time when Don Bayliss had been looking for one.

I was lucky: the lady in the first house I visited was the person I wanted. She also lived in Parkstone, not far from Mr Entwhistle. When Don had realised that the old man's bike had no lights, it would have been natural for him to walk the few hundred yards to Woking Road, where Mrs Adcock was selling a 'Carrera man's road bicycle, excellent condition, with essentials'.

She had to cast her mind back fifteen years but yes, Mrs Adcock said at last, she believed she sold her bike to a man who sounded a lot like the person I'd described. She remembered because of the cough and also because he seemed almost more interested in the lights than the bicycle itself.

I asked if she could remember anything else about their conversation.

Not really, she said.

Had he mentioned Hamworthy, for instance?

No.

Anywhere else?

No. But he did ask what the furthest distance was that the bicycle had been ridden in one go. He'd been very anxious about that, she remembered. 'Though to be honest with you,' she said, 'he didn't look fit enough to go very far.'

I thanked her, left her looking puzzled, and went back to the Ventry Arms and lay on my bed again. I was just beginning to see things in their proper relation to each other. I thought of Don setting off in the dark on his new bicycle with lights, cycling down to the Haven Hotel, ridding himself of his clothes – indeed, of his current life – sitting there smoking a forbidden cigarette, before climbing up the ladder to the bike racks, getting back on his bicycle and heading off again. But where to? Not to Hamworthy. Somewhere further off, perhaps much further. I thought of poor Don on the exercise bikes in the Marshall Worth gym trying to build up his fitness for the journey. I thought about him keeping his watch, to keep a close eye on the time. I felt I was close to understanding what had happened next if only I could think clearly, so I lay there, revolving details in my mind, turning them round to find the missing bit. After a while, I fished out my reports – the original witness statements, the Marshall Worth summary of Don's career and his bank account statements, the police summary of the Branksome and Westbourne break-ins, even

146

Mario's employment history – and read through them all again, carefully.

And at last I saw it.

At Lewisham Police Station there was confusion. On the phone, my contact had told me that Mario was still in custody but when I arrived I discovered he'd been released the day before without charge. The duty officer that night had been right: there hadn't been enough evidence to proceed.

I went first to Mario's place in Camberwell, the address he'd given to the station when he was discharged. As he'd told me, with that dismissive, louche pride of his, it was a respectable location, the top flat in a large Victorian terrace house not far from the nice cafés and bakeries on Peckham Road. But he wasn't there. Flossie was. Flossie looked about nineteen, a slender black woman who hadn't quite stopped being a girl yet. She wore a vest and micro shorts and chewed gum at me while I explained what I was doing. As soon as I mentioned Mario's name, she began a ferocious tirade against him. She'd had enough of him – and he knew better than to come to see her. The flat was not Mario's, it turned out, it was her family's, and her brothers would make sure Mario didn't treat her the way he'd treated the pregnant girl. I asked her if she thought Mario was responsible for the girl's death and she looked at me with scorn. She listed the girls he'd left in his wake: there were more than a few. With any girl it was only ever a question of when he would finally go too far. She became furious again and after that began to cry. No, she didn't know where he'd go now. Of course, some woman might be stupid enough to give him another chance. But not her.

I thanked her for her time and left, and so began my search round the various addresses Mario had given as the places where he liked to crash occasionally. I felt that Flossie was probably right, that there would be someone still prepared to trust him.

But I was wrong. He wasn't to be found anywhere. What I found instead was the same story from the different young women who answered the door to me, some of them with children clinging round their knees. Mario was more than a chancer, he was a fake, not the charmer with a pocketful of highs, but a mean, dishonest man with a bitter temper. More than one woman showed me old injuries. None of them doubted that he had pushed his pregnant girlfriend down that flight of steps. Many were frightened at the thought of him returning.

At eight o'clock, as the sun sank into Peckham, I'd run out of his likely boltholes, and there was only one address left to try, so I made my way to Holland Park and the family home of Dwight Fricker.

It was located in expensive St James's Gardens, opposite a church, a tall, ugly corner house the colour of mud, an eyesore in the midst of so much elegant white stucco. Perhaps Dwight Fricker would have called it 'honest'. The front facade was a monotonous expanse of wall with dull windows, a red door at the top of a flight of steps and a row of black railings. There was a car parked in front of the railings and as I crossed the road a guy got out and confronted me. I showed him Dwight Fricker's card and he showed me a blank face. I mentioned that I'd visited Dwight in Belmarsh a few days earlier and he looked suspicious. Finally, I said that I'd chatted to Dwight about painting – Kurelek, Montale and Dubuffet – and the mention of art seemed to intimidate him. He reluctantly made a call, then took me round the side of the house, where there was a second entrance. There I was met by another guy, who frisked me and asked me various questions. I told him that in Belmarsh Dwight had given me a message for his wife. He was dubious about that but seemed to consider me harmless, because after a further conversation with someone in the house he escorted me inside. Here, in the gloom of the dim high-ceilinged rooms, I saw Dwight

Fricker's paintings for the first time. They were shockingly bad, massive spoiled canvases of smears and gashes. One – called 'Sunrise' – depicted the fantasy creatures of nightmare, things with dripping fangs and insane eyes in curdled apocalyptic light, body parts scattered about. Some of these paintings reached the ceiling; others, smaller, leaned on the floor, their canvases turned to the wall, as if daring me to imagine what worse horrors they might contain. They did not horrify me, however; I wasn't sure why, but I'd have been tempted to say they were lacking in honesty. Fortunately no one asked my opinion. I was taken through a number of similar rooms, up a flight of stairs and into a sitting room, where a middle-aged woman waited by an empty fireplace. She had a pale face and hooded eyes and she regarded me with interest for what seemed like several minutes. There were none of Dwight's paintings in this room, I noticed. For a long time she said nothing. Then she ceased looking at me and spoke to the men.

'He's a cop,' she said.

I said I was a finder.

She ignored me. 'It's the way he looks about him. Pay attention,' she added, and one of the men started forward but she stopped him with a gesture of her hand.

'Did you see Dwight?' she asked me.

I said I'd seen him.

'How did he look?'

I told her he looked pretty good considering he'd just been released from the punishment cell, and she nodded.

'Dwight's indestructible,' she said.

At last she indicated a chair and dismissed her minders. She told me she was a businesswoman, with a number of strictly legal entertainment ventures and nothing extra on the side, unlike Dwight. She paid her taxes, she said, a fact I'd already discovered.

'So what's Dwight's message?' she asked.

'He thinks of you continually.'

She looked at me with those hooded eyes. 'Is that it?'

'Yes.'

'I can do without it,' she said at last. 'What do you really want?'

'Mario,' I said.

'What for?'

'Ask him a question about a man called Donald Bayliss.'

She thought about this.

'You've mistaken me for one Mario's girls, is that it?'

I said that Mario had nowhere else to go. He needed somewhere to hold up before he ran.

She didn't smile. 'Why will he run?'

'Because he's guilty, and sooner or later the Lewisham force will turn up the evidence.'

She looked at me deadpan and I realised that she knew where the evidence was. She was a woman who knew a lot, I thought.

I mentioned loyalty and again she looked at me for some time.

'What do you know about loyalty?' she asked.

I said I knew how it built up, sometimes unpredictably, how it persists past liking. 'Sometimes,' I said, 'obligations exist, even inconvenient ones with inconvenient people.'

'He's an annoying little prick,' she commented.

I agreed.

We sat in silence for a while.

'But he's not here,' she said. 'He knows better.'

I waited.

Some years before, she went on, Mario had made a comment to Dwight about her, and Dwight had taken it the wrong way. Dwight liked to take things the wrong way, she said, and in fact, she continued, she was surprised he hadn't taken me the wrong way when I met him in Belmarsh. But the point was that if Dwight ever found out Mario had showed up at the house, even to borrow a teabag, he wouldn't sleep until he'd arranged for him to be torn up and the bits thrown into the river.

'By the way,' she added, 'Dwight accepts no obligations. Obligations work entirely the other way with Dwight.'

I could see that, so I thanked her and took my leave.

'Ask them to let you out of the back.' she said. 'Then you won't have to look at those fucking horrible paintings.'

The man who escorted me out was hostile. Fricker's wife had bawled him out in front of me. He opened the door into the dark garden at the back and shoved me through it.

'You a finder?' he said. 'Find the fucking gate, you cunt.'

I felt my way along the path, found the gate, ignored it and went to stand in a shaft of moonlight, where anyone looking out would have a good view of me. The back of the house was just as ugly as the front, a muddy brown wall with the same perfunctory windows. In less than thirty seconds a blind went up on the second floor and Mario's face appeared looking out anxiously. He was reassuring himself that I'd left. It's very hard not to check that a danger has passed and I already knew that Mario had no self-control. He saw me straight away and I gestured at my watch and held up five fingers and he disappeared. I'd decided to wait five minutes before calling Lewisham, and just as I was getting out my phone, the back door opened and he limped down the steps, looking about him bleakly. I suspected he'd been asking Dwight's wife what he should do.

There was a bench against the garden wall invisible in

the shadows and I sat on it and Mario came up and stood there over me.

'I could fuck you up,' he said. 'Fuck you up and take off and you'd never catch up with me.'

I told him I wasn't interested in him, I was interested in Don Bayliss. But there was a lot about Don he'd neglected to tell me.

He thought about that; sat down.

'About the watch?'

'That's it.'

'You think I stole it from him?'

'No, I think he gave it to you. But not because he was going to kill himself.'

Mario looked at me and looked away, rubbed his chin anxiously. 'I can't stay here,' he said at last. 'I need a day, then I'm gone.'

I reminded him that I wasn't police. That I was paid only to find Don Bayliss.

He thought some more. He wasn't a fast thinker. 'So . . . I tell you what you want to know, you forget all about me. That right?'

I told him he was one of the most forgettable people I'd ever met, and he wasn't sure how to take that; he grimaced and rubbed his chin a bit more, and at last said he could give me five minutes. But to tell me what had happened in 2008, he had to go further back, he said, to 2005, one morning at the beginning of July. He'd been in London, sorting out some business. A little before nine he was on his way to see some guy in Barking. Later, he was going to meet a girl in town. It was a standard London day, nothing sort of weather, road works at Spitalfields, traffic backed all the way up Bishopsgate, people, litter, pigeons, the usual things, broken escalator, crowded Tube train. He was only going one stop, getting out at Aldgate. Then, suddenly, he was somewhere else, not on the Tube train, there wasn't a train anymore, everything was lopsided and grey, the air soupy and foul, dark shapes moving slowly through it, as if underwater, and he lay there, squashed underneath the debris of other people. There was that angry, numb sound deafness makes. He didn't know how long he'd been there but it dawned on him at last that a bomb had gone off. There seemed to be some people still alive and he thought he might be one of them, though he wasn't sure, he couldn't move or speak and he knew there was something badly wrong: he groped around with his hand and couldn't find his right leg.

He stopped talking, pulled up his trouser cuff and showed me his prosthetic.

'Thought it might slow me down,' he said. 'Turns out the girls like it.'

A memory came to me of something Mrs Bayliss had said the first time we met.

'Don Bayliss found you,' I said.

He nodded.

Don had been on the same train, in the adjoining carriage. Mario was first aware of him as a pair of hands. Then a voice. 'Stay still.' It had been difficult to hear him because he was still deaf, Don had to put his mouth very close to Mario's ear; Mario still remembered the feel of Don's lips and the sound of the words as if they were physical things Don was folding up and gently pushing into his bleeding ears. It was then he began to really panic, to think he was going to die. Last moments. Thoughts of his life, a childhood memory, his mother's hands grey and mauve on her hips. Don was calm and busy. He looked like a benign scoutmaster, the soft-bodied kind whose uniforms are always a little too tight. In fact, Don's jacket and shirt were torn, and his face was streaked with dirt and blood, but he gave the impression of knowing what he was doing. He did know. He made a tourniquet out of what was left of his shirt and tied it round Mario's left thigh and waited with him until the paramedics arrived.

Don had been first-aider at Marshall Worth, of course, and health-and-safety coordinator of the water-sports youth club.

'Saved my life,' Mario said. 'That's what they told me. Without the tourniquet, I would've bled to death.' Don had visited him a few times in the hospital. They talked, telling each other a bit about themselves; Mario in particular opened up. He had a sentimental side, of course. Having his life saved had been miraculous, an epiphany, a high to top all his other highs. Naturally, it had no lasting effect on him. Soon he left hospital, picked up his old life, started to forget about Don. But three years later, out of the blue, Don reappeared.

'Back end of September, he came to the club. A dead night midweek, Wednesday I think. Looking like a wreck. He wasn't interested in the girls, they embarrassed him. I knew straight away he'd come to ask me for something.' He laughed to himself. 'It was quite a surprise.'

He waited a moment to tease me but I'd had enough of him and I spoiled it.

'He asked you if you could get him a passport.'

He looked at me sourly.

'First offence, counterfeiting,' I said. At first I hadn't noticed it in Mario's record but it jumped out at me when I looked again. Yes, Mario admitted. Don wanted a passport – and he was only too pleased to help. After all, they had an affinity, they had 'shared time' in that death-filled train carriage. It took another few Wednesday nights getting all the necessaries from Don but in the end a passport was obtained and in due course Mario went down to Bournemouth and handed it to him in a seaside café in the early afternoon of 30 October. A horrible little café, Mario said, like something from the past, and Don had kept him waiting, in fact he'd been so late that Mario thought he wasn't going to show at all and had sent him a text from the café – Don had given him a new number – saying that if he wasn't there soon he was going back to London. He'd actually been on the point of leaving when Don called him to say he was on his way, and when he arrived he was in a terrible funk, hardly able to string two words together, he just took the passport and sat there in silence, and Mario left. But, anyway, Mario said, if I knew about the passport already why was I bothering him about it?

'Because I want to know what name it was in.'

He didn't remember. He'd given Don a choice, three or four names he had on the books at the time.

I waited.

He shook his head. 'All I remember's the first name, he went for it straight away, like it meant something to him.'

'Was it Adrian?'

He looked at me sourly again.

I had one last question, I said. *Why* did Don want a passport? Now he was indignant. Naturally, he'd never asked, he had too much consideration for the man who'd saved his life. But, he added, it was obvious Don had done something bad. It wasn't just that he looked guilty, that he was so clearly desperate, he was throwing everything away, his lovely life, his top job, his big house, his wife. Why would anyone give all that up if they absolutely didn't have to? 'Don had done something. He had to run, and fast.' Mario shook his head in wonder. 'People,' he said, with that amiable smile.

I would get no more out of him now except more self-serving theatrics, and I got to my feet and walked away towards the gate.

He shouted after me. He never wanted to hear from me again, he said.

I let myself out and stood on the pavement. It was ten o'clock. The whole sky was the same mineral grey, finely textured like the surface of a smooth pebble. It calmed me. I called Lewisham and told them where Mario was, then began to walk towards Shepherd's Bush.

It was midnight when I reached the Ventry Arms. As I stepped out of the taxi, the avenue was quiet with that soft but somehow dull quietness of warm summer nights; I could smell blossoms and pine and, more faintly, the sea. It was so inviting I almost set off to walk, as once before, along that lane through the woods of the chine to the bluff overlooking the beach, but it was late and I turned instead into the inn. Most lights were off, there was no one about except the night receptionist, and I'd taken my key and was making my way towards the stairs when I noticed a light still on in the bar, and I looked in. Mac sat there nursing an empty glass.

She said, 'I thought if I waited long enough you'd find me.'

Too late I remembered our dinner date.

Embarrassed, I went towards her and she made a gesture at once absolving and regretful, and we looked at each other for a moment in that cautiously exploratory way the newly discovered have. I said that I could at least buy her another drink and she held up her glass and I took it from her. She was wearing, I noticed with another pang of guilt, not her usual tracksuit, but a blue summer dress printed with white flowers. I could smell the scent she was wearing.

Although it was late, neither of us was tired. We talked at first, naturally enough, about books, the classics mainly, describing the authors we loved best, how their voices spoke to us across the years, how it was that their manners might be strange but their tone so personal it was as if they spoke to us like people we knew, or even like versions of ourselves. Gradually the day fell from me, and with it the memory of Mario. Mac's voice was lower than I remembered; as we talked it seemed to get even deeper and I watched her mouth as she spoke. She asked me what had made me a reader and I told her I'd always been greedy for other people's stories; and I asked her in turn why she read.

'To feel less alone,' she said.

We talked then about ourselves. She wanted to know about my childhood in Baghdad and I told her what I could remember and what seemed to make sense, which was perhaps not much, and also about my schooldays in Paris, when I lived first with an uncle, then with a paid companion, and how I loved especially to ride on the Métro, particularly during rush hour, to feel myself part of the press of people, the human flow. In turn, she told me about her childhood in Tuatapere. She pointed out how different we were. Growing up, I'd had so much other life in my life, and she so little. As a child, I'd had people, cities, civilisation, history, all around me, stretching back centuries and into the future. She'd had nothing but mountains and sea, a river plain, the sky. At first, she said, it suited her, she loved to run along the trails, to feel alone in the great inhuman scene, it made her more herself; but later, gradually, she began to feel uneasy, too weak to hold on to anything for long in those vast spaces, as if she were a seed at the mercy of the wind; and she became afraid she could be carried off into a sort of oblivion, and in fact lose herself, as people are lost in the oblivion of death. For a long time, while she ran, the sheer movement and momentum of running protected her: the palpable pump of her heart in her chest, the suck of her lungs, kept her together. Then one day it didn't. The fuss about the Olympics raised a breeze, it plucked her up and spun her suddenly away, helpless, out of control, no longer who she'd been. So she'd wedged herself into that janitor's cupboard in Athens airport and begun to read, to be with other people in their stories and so find herself again.

Her voice had changed once more, coloured by emotion, it was deeper again and somehow nearer, and I seemed to hear it even after she had fallen silent, and I watched her smile again, wondering what colour her eyes were, previously I'd thought grey, now they sometimes seemed brown, sometimes hazel, beautiful and sad, and I felt that falling away of other things, and that quickening of the body and its interest, and recognised it for what it was.

I said that missing people lived so vividly in the minds of others that I often felt that we don't properly exist except in our relationships, of which we are the result.

She asked if that was the case with the person I was trying to find now, and I said that there were few people I'd talked to who hadn't been touched by him in some way or other, in particular by his disappearance. In a sense, I said, it is always in the minds of others where a missing person is finally found.

'Of course,' she said, 'there are many ways to be alone.'

And, sometimes, ways to come together again, I said, after a moment.

She smiled.

'Two people in an after-hours bar,' she said, 'talking.'

Her voice seemed nearer than ever, she herself seemed closer though she hadn't moved, and I was aware of her smiling mouth and her beautiful, sad eyes and her pretty cotton dress so flimsy in her lap, and her hands, one of which, as I watched, moved across the table and I put out my own and our fingers brushed together and held.

Grey light coming through the window woke us and we lay there listening to each other's breathing. She spoke first.

She was married, she said, she had a husband in New Zealand. She apologised for lying. She didn't want to leave Bournemouth without telling me. Her husband was a man from whom she could have secrets but she thought I was not. He was a writer, fifteen years older than her. She had met him on one of his book tours. Ten years after the mess of the Athens Olympics, she'd been living in Wellington, training young runners for the regional athletics association, living alone in a clapboard bungalow on the edge of Johnsonville and her future husband came to talk at the local bookshop. He was funny and wise and, she thought, perhaps a little lonely too, and after the talk and the applause and the signings were over, she went up and asked him if he was married. Six months later they had a civil wedding in Auckland and lived there now in a modest house called (by previous occupants who were evidently Tolkien fans) 'Bag End'. Her voice was a murmur in the quiet of the night, carefully explaining these things to me, or perhaps to herself. Beware writers, she said. They're not like readers, they live solitary lives in their own books. And they really don't do anything but write. Every year, as the New Zealand summer turned to autumn and her husband concentrated on finishing a new book before his deadline, she felt the need to get away from the silent house in which she was only a bystander, to be herself, perhaps to find herself again, which is how people usually described it, though she might just as well call it losing herself, or, better still, to feel herself once more that girl running the trails in the nothingness of mountains and sea, before she was afraid of it, when she was neither lost nor found but simply, unselfconsciously, in the world. Though, she added, it was dangerous to do this.

I asked why.

Because, she said, one day she would decide not to go back.

We lay there in silence after she'd said all this. I said that in a sense I too was married, I had a wife and also a son, and though they were dead my life remained an accommodation with my memories of them, or some of the memories, which persisted intensely without reason, and were so much a part of who I was that I could never lose myself or indeed find myself. I was not alone and could never be.

I could tell she was wondering whether or not to ask me more about my wife and my son and their deaths, and in the end deciding against it.

Perhaps you are trying to find *them*, she said.

Perhaps, I replied. Though of course they are not lost but dead.

'Then perhaps it's yourself you're looking for after all,' she said after a moment.

We lay there without talking until the room was filled with light, when I got dressed and left.

Now that we knew about the passport, things were different, processes speeded up. A few necessary days passed, requests went out, information came in, a fair amount of what had been hidden was finally revealed and soon I was pressing the buzzer at Sunrise and announcing myself and watching the gates swing slowly open again. It was another sunny, fresh afternoon in Bournemouth and the garden had a sort of magazine perfection not to be wasted on someone like me who had no interest in it. As usual, Sylvia met me at the front door. There were minor things I still did not know, and some things I did not want to mention, and still other things – the motive, for instance – which as yet I could only guess at; but I had told her on the phone that now, at least, I knew with a degree of certainty what had happened fifteen years earlier on the day Don disappeared. She greeted me gravely and led me into the house and we sat in our usual fashion on our respective sofas in the living room.

I asked her to bear with me while I narrated the sequence of events and she looked at me without speaking.

Don hadn't been sure until the very last moment that he was going to go through with what he'd planned, I said. Before his early afternoon meeting he'd received an ultimatum from the person he'd arranged to meet off-site. Now, in the boardroom, with the meeting running late, it was already long past the time when he should have left. At a quarter past two he had to make a decision one way or the other. He decided, and got up, and left the boardroom. From somewhere discreet, probably the toilets nearby, he used a new phone to call the person he was going to meet, then, in as normal a manner as possible, he left the building and hurried down to the East Cliff Café on the front, where, at three o'clock, a little before Gregory Barrett encountered him there, he met the man called Mario, whom I had already mentioned, who handed him a passport in the name of Adrian Palmer.

Sylvia made a noise. Her face was a peculiar colour. I continued.

When Don had his passport he went to buy a second-hand

bicycle with some of the cash he'd carefully withdrawn in several tiny amounts over many months: he was anxious there should be no record of any purchases with his card. For the same reason he was also anxious that the bicycle should already have lights – he was going to ride it in the dark – so when he realised that Mr Entwhistle's bike had none he moved on at once to Mrs Adcock in Woking Road whose bicycle turned out to fit the bill.

I paused again. Sylvia sat looking at me as she might an intruder. I was anxious not to anger her, at least not before I finished my story, though I could not expect to avoid upsetting her.

I told her I couldn't account exactly for the few hours that followed while Don waited for nightfall. Wherever he'd been, he'd managed to change his clothes. And when it was dark, at about six o'clock, he cycled down to the Haven Hotel at the mouth of the harbour and threw the bag containing his old clothes and his old phone up on to the ledge above the walkway. The only items he didn't pack in the bag were his old watch, which he had given to Mario in the café, his new phone and his new watch, which he needed for the next stages of his journey. Then he smoked a cigarette and at some point before eight, when the last of the lobstermen came in, retrieved the bicycle from the car park and cycled off to Southampton.

Sylvia gave a short bark not to be mistaken for a laugh. 'Southampton? Don couldn't have cycled to the end of our drive.'

Don had prepared, I explained. He'd talked to a young colleague about distances so he could calculate how long the journey might take him, visited the Marshall Worth gym at lunchtimes to build up his fitness. It's thirty-five miles from Bournemouth to Southampton, generally flat going. His young colleague would have taken no more than, say, three hours. Don made it in nine, cycling steadily through the night. He knew it would be worth it: the police would be unlikely to check transport hubs beyond the Bournemouth, Poole and Christchurch areas.

Sylvia said she found all this difficult to believe. I handed her a printout of a CCTV image from the forecourt of Southampton coach station. Fortunately for my purposes, between the months of September and October 2008 there had been an ongoing police inquiry into the persistent vandalism of coaches there, and, as standard procedure, CCTV images from the forecourt had been archived in the police database, where they remained. This image, taken at five o'clock on the morning of 31 October, showed a queue of people waiting with their luggage to board the early airline bus, and at the back was a dishevelled, overweight man in a tracksuit with a small backpack.

169

Sylvia was still fighting it. The image was poor, she said, the man at the back of the queue could be anyone. I handed her another printout. On it was the reproduction of a page in a passport and the details of a check-in registered at Gatwick North Terminal at nine o'clock on 31 October. The name of the traveller was Adrian Palmer but the face in the passport was unmistakably Don's, familiar and jowly, looking slightly startled; and Sylvia stared at it for a long time, saying nothing.

'Where did he fly to?' she said at last in a changed voice.

'Lima, Peru.'

Bewilderment shook her.

'Why?' she said. 'He doesn't know anyone in Peru,' she added.

I did not know. I said that I had come to the end of my knowledge of Don Bayliss's journey. We had, of course, been in contact with the authorities in Lima but, after his arrival at the airport, Adrian Palmer had left no trace anywhere in Peru. We only knew that there was no record of him leaving the country. South America is a large area with unusually porous national borders and lax ID regulations – and an obvious place to go for those wanting to evade justice, though I did not mention this to Sylvia. I added only a few words of explanation about Mario, to tie up some loose ends. As I'd already explained, he was the man who had met Don a few times at the table-dancing club Taboo. But, I told her, they had first met in the 7/7 bombings in London, when Don had saved Mario's life. He owed Don a favour, which Don had eventually called in.

She sat there in silence.

'Is he alive?' she asked at last.

I said I didn't know.

'What happens now?'

I said other agencies would take over the matter. I doubted that I would be asked to continue in any capacity. Although I had not found Don, I had found out what had happened to him on the day he disappeared.

All her self-control fell away. It was like watching the collapse of an ice cliff into the Arctic Ocean. She began to breathe in short, harsh gasps.

'Why?' she said. 'Why did he do it?'

I made no reply. For the obvious reasons, motives are generally the slowest things to pin down, and I did not want to speculate on the possible meanings of Don's break-ins at Ronald Phipps's house or the Forsters', or on Don's relationship with the fourteen-year-old Lucia, or on Don weeping at the sight of a newspaper story about the elopement of another fourteen-year-old girl, or anything else of possible interest.

'He left me,' Sylvia said abruptly. She had seized, as we

do, on the incontrovertible, no matter how painful. That's how much he'd thought of her, she said. Not only to leave her but to hide his leaving from her, to give her the pain of believing he had killed himself, to leave her *with his death*, with the years of imagining his suffering, of feeling guilty, of questioning herself, when all the time in fact he would be alive, elsewhere, knowing that she remained in the dark. He was always a coward, she said bitterly, always avoided confrontation, left her to deal with problems alone, with the trauma of her miscarriage for instance, after which, in fact, she'd faced such difficulties while he thrived, selfishly concentrated on his career, it had suited him not to be bothered with a family, and he'd never even thought about her pain, he was that sort of man, she said, selfish, yes, never reaching out to her, withdrawing, squeezing the joy out of everything. And other people didn't realise what he was really like, she said, they liked him, they didn't like her, she knew that too. People at Marshall Worth were always praising him to her, his team in the office, the CEO, those stupid people in America, Sol whatever-his-name-was, others he used to meet, they'd send him presents after he'd been over there, once they'd sent them tickets for a box at Covent Garden to see the ballet. She detested ballet! Nice Don, clever Don, friendly Don. They had no idea what he was really like, spoilt, thoughtless, passive, weak, unsupportive, self-indulgent . . . She ran out of breath and sat there panting.

I remained silent, not sure if she had more to say but anxious to give her the opportunity to say it all, however true or untrue, for it was all real to her.

'He never loved me,' she said at last and began to cry. She sat crying, her handsome face ugly, looking small and lost on the massive sofa. This too was what Don Bayliss had done. She had no more to say. And after a few moments I got up and without saying goodbye quietly let myself out.

Two days later, to my surprise, I flew to New York. I hadn't even had a chance to check out of the Ventry Arms. It seemed the story was not quite over. A conversation with Louise had resulted in a change of heart. My report already contained enough new information to justify her appointment of a finder, for which she was receiving some praise, but she sensed the possibility of a bigger win, something to really grab the attention of senior figures. I had mentioned to her some loose thoughts about Don's reason for going to Peru, and she at once managed to secure some extra budget.

From Newark airport I took a taxi into Manhattan, where I checked into the Best Western on West 48th, and showered before walking to Marshall Worth's temporary headquarters on Madison Avenue. The company was squatting here in a modest brownstone skyscraper not above fifteen storeys high, while waiting for their futuristic new headquarters to be constructed on Fifth. I thought in fact that the unglamorous building suited Sol Abramowitz, whom I met in his office on the tenth floor. He was tiny and stringy with a wide, unfinished face and outsized voice. Even his small talk was high-energy, and he spent some time now, as before, praising and mourning Don, 'a true English gentleman'.

The downward view from his window was cranes and gantries, trucks and pick-ups, the outward view nothing but cloudless blue.

By the way, he said, abruptly switching his manner, as he had done once before, there would be no conversation about the internal inquiry into Don which we'd discussed, none. I said that in fact I wanted to talk about something else completely: Don's home life.

He spread his arms, gave a wide smile. Don loved it, he said. It was everything to him, the house, the garden, 'Mrs Don' above all.

That was interesting. I asked about Mrs Don.

But when pressed to remember what Don had told him, he couldn't; it turned out that Don had told him very little, he'd been dutiful but extremely minimal. Sol had the vague impression that Mrs Bayliss was a wife very like his own – quiet and graceful, soft-voiced, a kind and comforting presence.

I asked if he'd remembered anything else about Don that he wanted to share. Anything Don might have said to him that sounded unexpected? Sol thought about that, and after a moment remembered a conversation he'd had with Don on that fishing trip in Connecticut. They'd been sitting round the fire with a drink talking about themselves. What were their early ambitions? If they hadn't gone into finance, what careers might they have had? Sol had said that he'd always wanted to be an oceanographer; if he hadn't failed to get the grades at high school, that's what he would have been. But Don, he said, hadn't liked the question at all, it made him uncomfortable. He told Sol he'd spent a lot of his teenage years hanging aimlessly round bars and pool halls without any sense of purpose or ambition; if he hadn't met Sylvia, he would've ended up a bum. I remembered Ronald Phipps saying that Don had told him the same thing.

It was time to meet a few of Sol's colleagues. I'd asked him to introduce me to everyone still working for the company who had met Don regularly in New York, and Sol had gathered them together in a meeting room down the corridor.

There were only three of them, all in their late forties,

all wearing business suits: Sophie Chodosh, a brisk Jewish woman with thick-rimmed glasses and dark hair scraped back; Kurt Halmann, still looking like the all-American college boy he must have been fifteen years earlier; and Ellen Brown, the sort of quiet person who waits till everyone else has spoken before giving her view. Sophie had for several years been Don's direct liaison in the New York accountancy office; Kurt was part of the team that worked on a daily basis with the international hubs, particularly the UK; and Ellen coordinated specific one-off projects with international involvement. All had met Don on a number of occasions in New York, and Kurt and Ellen had also met him once or twice on trips to the UK.

Their memories were excellent, they were articulate and thoughtful people and they'd liked and respected Don. But they told me almost nothing of interest. They repeated in slightly different forms what others had already told me many times before. Don had been the quintessential English gentleman. Polite. Well-mannered. Sophie remembered that if he was sitting when a woman came into the room he always stood to greet her. Also, Ellen added, he held open the door for women to let them go through first. Kurt remembered how courteous Don was in his conversation, never impatient or dismissive, not even raising his voice. None of them had thought Don a likely suicide:

his death had shocked them. There had been suicides in the New York office but no one expected there to be any in England. The English always seemed so steady, so unflappable, so undemonstrative, and Don more English than most. But this, Ellen said, was to downplay or even trivialise the very real mental health problems caused by the pressures brought about by the financial crash. They agreed it had been a desperate time.

All of this was interesting but unilluminating.

Had they ever talked to Don about his home life?

They hadn't. Sophie and Ellen hadn't even known that he was married.

Could they imagine Don deliberately doing something wrong?

They absolutely couldn't.

Could they imagine him breaking the law?

They looked at me dumbfounded.

So I thanked them for their time, received their recommendations for restaurants to try while I was in Manhattan, and returned to Sol.

'Find what you were looking for?'

'Not yet.'

I asked him if there were any other New York colleagues Don had worked with. Not in the building, Sol said. And maybe not anywhere.

I asked him instead who had organised Don's itineraries when he visited New York. There must have been someone who scheduled his meetings, organised his travel, arranged his accommodation and so on. Sol said his PA would have handled all that. And it was true that they would have seen a lot of Don when he was over. Having said that, over the years he'd naturally had a number of PAs; nearly all of them had since left Marshall Worth. He had no idea where they might be now. I could tell he was coming to the end of his patience with me.

To narrow it down, I asked him if any of his former PAs had got on particularly well with Don, and he sat there for a moment thinking. There was a lady called Francesca, he said, very bouncy, a lot of fun, she and her husband were great outdoor enthusiasts and had eventually moved to Alaska to work in conservation a few years before the crash.

I shook my head. Anyone else?

A lady called Petra, old-school, rather severe. Don had liked her. She'd stayed on past retirement age and was almost seventy when she left the company sometime in the mid-noughties.

'No,' I said.

There was briefly a young man called Brian.

'No.'

He sat there thinking.

'Anyone from Peru?'

He stared at me, shook his head. But there was another lady, he forgot her name, Jewish like himself, used to bake muffins for the office. She'd been Sol's PA when the crash happened.

I asked him to tell me more about her.

She hadn't been particularly memorable. Nice lady. Good-natured. Not ambitious to move on, like so many PAs. Got a little flustered in meetings. Her aunt had left her an apartment in Sutton Place, he seemed to remember. She was short-sighted, had a habit of peering at you while you were speaking to her. She made little mistakes and laughed in embarrassment. Don had praised her muffins. Her name, he remembered at last, was Sarah. Sarah something.

'This can't be the sort of stuff you're after,' he said.

I asked what happened to Sarah.

He thought again. She'd quit after the crash, later that year sometime.

To join another company?

'No,' Sol said. 'To have a baby.'

There is often a moment in an investigation of this kind, at the end, when I'm not sure whether I want to actually find the missing person. To cause havoc. To arrive in their lives like the avenging angel of history, to expose them to the past, to the world, not least to the people they have left behind, to confront them with the person they used to be. But such confrontation between our different selves is, consciously or unconsciously, an inescapable part our existence, as Robert Louis Stevenson realised when he wrote *Jekyll and Hyde*. And so I stood in Sackett Street in Brooklyn, waiting only for the right moment.

Number 437 was a three-storey townhouse at the end of a long terrace row of similar houses in reddish-brown brick in the Carroll Gardens district. The hot afternoon simmered on the tarmac. Trees along the street cast their flimsy shade, and the little stores nearby, selling picture frames or electrical equipment, stood with their doors open. Noises came from a nearby school and a playground round the corner. Visible in the distance were the improbable towers of Manhattan wobbling in the heat haze like a mirage, but here things were close and ordinary, children's voices, graffiti, the jabber of small birds. Number 437 had been painted in pastel colours and the door at the top of the stoop was a bright cheerful red, and I crossed the street and knocked on it.

A middle-aged lady answered.

'Sarah?'

'Yes?'

She was wearing jeans and a shapeless T-shirt and her hair was an untidy grey nest. From inside the house I could hear the accelerating spin cycle of a washing machine begin.

'Is Adrian home?'

She peered at me in the blindish way of short-sighted people and her face slowly flushed. Perhaps it was my accent.

'He's out at the gym.' The flush spread all the way down her throat. 'What do you want?'

'I've been trying to find him,' I said, 'since he went missing in 2008.'

For a moment she didn't move or speak, her eyes seemed to glaze over. 'I always knew it would happen one day,' she said. 'You better come in.'

We picked our way down a hallway narrowed by clutter – crates from a grocery store, fallen coats, an ironing board, a bicycle – and went into a sitting room equally dishevelled. I sat on a peeling leather sofa piled with school exercise books and Sarah perched on the edge of a rocking chair. Around us was the common family mess: laundry, magazines and comics, sports kit, unhung pictures, a half-finished jigsaw. Sarah looked round at it. They'd given up clearing away after she had Ruth, she said.

I asked her how many children she and Don had.

'Four. Zach, Reuben, Sol and Ruth.' She drew my attention to a photograph above the fireplace. 'Fourteen, eleven, nine and seven.' In the photograph the four children had linked arms, laughing. None looked like Don Bayliss, who stood behind them with his arm round Sarah, a smaller, balder man than he had been, also laughing. Sarah was still looking at the mess. 'Sometimes, I think Don's the worst.' She smiled. 'It's funny calling him Don again. Of course, I never do anymore. It takes me back to the first few years. Are you police?'

I explained.

'I suppose,' she went on, 'you'll want to know everything. How does it work? Do you have a tape recorder?'

I told her I didn't need to record anything. Nor to hear her story unless she wanted to tell me.

She would tell me something, she said, so I would understand it from her point of view. When she graduated from college she'd drifted into admin roles in a variety of local businesses. She wasn't ambitious, had no strong interests or particular talents. She wanted to be in New York simply because she'd grown up there. Everywhere she worked, she was the least energetic and incisive person in the group. Perhaps it should have bothered her but she accepted it. She had an inheritance from an aunt which gave her a financial security that most secretaries wouldn't have. At first she had a vague idea she'd meet someone, a co-worker, and start a family, but it didn't happen; and in time she wasn't sure she wanted it to happen.

'I was never very desirable,' she said matter-of-factly. 'Girlfriends tell you otherwise but you always know the truth.'

In 2006, she got the job at Marshall Worth, PA to the Vice President and Head of Internal Affairs, a big deal for her, a move into a different kind of business, sharper, more demanding. The first few months were terrifying. Sol was fair but tough. She was easily flustered, made silly mistakes. Quite soon after she started, about four months in, she was told to make arrangements for the visit of a Vice President from the United Kingdom. This made her more nervous than ever: an important guest from overseas. From the beginning things went wrong, she said. The flight was cancelled, the hotel lost the booking. She forgot to amend his schedule with a last-minute change and Don missed his first meeting. It was all a disaster. By the time she finally met him he had every reason to be furious with her.

She began to cry. She didn't apologise or explain, just sat there, head bowed, silently weeping until she was able to go on.

Don had come into her booth, this bald, overweight, middle-aged guy in a terrible suit, and presented her with a box of chocolates. To thank her, he said. He was sorry she'd had so many difficult things to deal with.

She wiped her face.

At the end of that first trip he'd taken her out for dinner to thank her for everything, to a restaurant she'd never have dared go to on her own.

She looked at me. 'Ever fallen in love?'

I said that I had and saw that she believed me.

A couple of years passed. Each year Don came to New York three or four times. She arranged his itineraries, he would take her out to a restaurant. When she discovered

185

she was pregnant she didn't tell him. He was married, of course. He never spoke about his wife but she could not imagine Don confronting her with this situation. She handed in her notice, prepared to start a different kind of life. With her inheritance, she could bring up a child quite comfortably on her own, it would be, in fact, the easiest, least complicating – least compromising – thing to do. Don could continue his life in England. So she decided not to tell him, to leave Marshall Worth, to disappear. But then the crash happened, she was persuaded to stay on an extra week and Don flew in unexpectedly for an emergency meeting. So of course he saw her condition. Even then, she still expected to be a single mother. They barely talked about it. She said that if I'd learned anything about Don during my search for him I would know that he was not the sort of person to step forward straight away. So Don flew back to the UK, she left Marshall Worth, sold her aunt's house in Sutton Place and bought the townhouse in Brooklyn, began ante-natal classes. She missed Don but knew it was for the best. It was a shock when, one late November night, she opened the door of her apartment and found him standing there.

'He was wearing this tracksuit, badly stained, and he was dirty. One of his shoes was broken, he had a cut over his left eye and his breath stank of cigarettes. He looked like a homeless guy. He told me that's what he was. I thought I would never again know such happiness.'

There was the sound of the front door being unlocked and she stopped talking and we waited together in silence listening to the bumping and breathing in the hallway; then the footsteps came nearer and Don Bayliss stood at the end of the room, looking at me. He was sixty-five years old, no longer stout but small and softly shapeless. The folds of his face had slipped down and lay loose on his throat. His head was entirely bald and very shiny.

Sarah said, 'This gentleman's from England.'

Don nodded. 'I thought you might be.' He had a quiet, mumbly voice. He gave a little shrug, a small staggering shuffle as if caught off balance. 'It's the way you look about you, I think. What are you, police?'

'A finder,' I said.

He nodded again.

Sarah went over and embraced him for a long, quiet moment, then left the room, and Don and I looked at each other.

'I don't want to go back,' he said.

'It may not be your choice,' I replied.

He took Sarah's place on the rocking chair and after a moment began to talk.

★

What he'd done that October in 2008 was astonishing to him now. He was a timid person, he said. Passive. It really wasn't the sort of thing he would do.

His voice as he spoke was low and hesitant, a soft rummaging of English vowels. He would say something and fall silent, frowning, as if regretting having said it, and after a moment start to revise it. In this way he talked me through his disappearance, nearly all of which I already knew, some of which he'd forgotten himself. I had to remind him how he sat on the rocks under the ledge at the Haven Hotel smoking a last cigarette before his night ride to Southampton. He remembered the ride. A nightmare, he said. He'd been in poor physical shape despite his attempts to prepare. His cough was particularly bad. His back was sore, despite Rose's attention. Setting off along the unlit, deserted beach front to Southbourne a little after eight he'd felt the strangeness of what he was doing so vividly he had to stop to be sick. In Christchurch he fell and cut his face on the kerb. The A35 seemed endless, long and narrow and dark under trees as he pedalled with excruciating slowness through the New Forest, buffeted from time to time by the occasional overnighting truck thundering past. Exhausted, he fell again just beyond Lyndhurst and thought he might not be able to go on. He had the airline bus to catch, he kept checking his progress on his new watch and knew he was not doing well. At last he came to Southampton. But after dumping the bike in the river at the port, he still had to jog the last half-mile to the coach station to get there on time. He was in a terrible state. Even on the coach he couldn't relax and not long after boarding he had a panic attack. To his horror, the driver stopped on the hard shoulder and for a while Don thought he was going to be ejected. At Gatwick, as Mario had said, things were smoother. The big international airports have the least stringent checks. There were no problems getting through passport control. Gradually, he was lulled almost into thinking he was just an ordinary traveller. Lima was strange, of course, also the two-week-long onward overland journey, arranged by associates of Mario, up through Central America and across the border into the US. But nothing had been so hard as that cycle ride at the beginning.

As he paused in his reminiscence the obvious unanswered questions rose into his mind and he met my eyes.

'Sarah was pregnant,' he said. 'That's why.'

As an explanation, this was so obviously inadequate that I did not need to point it out. He winced as he looked at me and he turned away and his eyes went to the family photograph on the wall.

He asked me if I had children and I told him I used to have a son, and he nodded.

He'd been a useless, aimless person, he said, diffident, passive; he didn't know what to do with himself; Sylvia had taken him in hand but the feeling of emptiness remained. Until she got pregnant, he said. Suddenly, to his surprise, he felt different. He was going to be a father; he finally made sense to himself. He bought baby things, toys and clothes, and sewed labels into them, and for a few months thought about little else.

'Then Sylvia miscarried,' he said.

He sat for a while in silence. Sylvia was always good at dealing with things, personal things, he said, him not so much. They were both emotional but her emotion made her turn to practical matters, things she could do or not do, his seemed to choke him, he couldn't even speak about them. One day he came home from work and she'd put all the baby things in the attic. She'd decided, she told him, not to have children.

'Her decision,' he said. 'Her body, her pain. Not mine. It wasn't my place to argue against her. Besides, I never used to argue.'

At first he thought that his emptiness would go away. But it didn't. He thought he would stop thinking about children but he didn't; instead, the thoughts grew stronger, became obsessive.

I told him that I'd come across his copy of *Mrs Dalloway*

with the underlined passage in it. Yes, he said, someone had mentioned to him that Virginia Woolf had no children and felt the lack, and he read the book to see if she discussed living with the unhappiness of it but she didn't, she discussed only other sorts of unhappiness; and he got to wondering if he'd ever be distressed enough to kill himself, as Septimus does in the novel, or as Virginia Woolf herself did. He didn't think so. But he thought about Septimus quite a bit, the idea that he had a hidden part of himself, and not just hidden but truer and more vulnerable than the rest of him. That's how he felt himself about his secret longing for children. Sylvia was strong but he was weak, all he could do with his distress was hide it.

'I was always good at hiding things,' he said.

He'd creep upstairs to the attic when Sylvia was out and look at the baby toys and clothes and imagine what it would be like if Adrian had lived, if he'd come home with them, what it would be like to hold him, smell him, listen to him breathing, watch him sleeping in his cot.

I said it was interesting how often what we do begins by imagining it. The idea of ourselves watching a sleeping child, for instance.

Don threw me a glance and started to squeeze his hands together, his knuckles whitening. He took a deep breath. One day, he said, he'd seen Ronald's granddaughter asleep in her pushchair by their pool and felt a rush of something, something overwhelming, a tenderness. He remembered sitting on his lounger staring at her, listening to her breathe, he could feel his face smiling, his eyes getting wet, and for a moment his pain went away completely.

'Not even my own child,' he said. 'But it made me feel . . .'

He sighed.

'I'm a numbers man,' he said. 'I can't explain.'

He couldn't explain what he did either. Once he'd noticed that Ronald's patio doors didn't close properly he couldn't stop thinking about the baby inside, he was seized by something he'd never felt before, an overwhelming compulsion, an utter disregard of risks, and one night he found himself, the most timid person he knew, creeping into Ronald's house, climbing the stairs and tiptoeing past the rooms where the rest of the family lay in bed, along the landing into the little room at the end to watch a child sleeping in her cot. It was bizarre, he said, he became strange to himself, but at the same time he felt himself more fully who he really was. Afterwards he felt ashamed, he told himself never again, but in fact there was another occasion. At Hamworthy, where he helped run a youth water-sports club, he saw the little brother of one of the teenagers sleeping in his pram – a baby boy, like Adrian! – and when he visited his father's home to return something the older girl had left behind, he saw they had the same defective patio doors as Ronald. The compulsion seized him again. To break into this stranger's house was an even more reckless thing to do but he was helpless to resist the temptation, and he went there one night, and got in easily and went boldly upstairs, as if protected by the charm of his obsession, even stopping to close a bedroom door on the way, and into the room at the end, and sat there for an hour or more, gazing at the sleeping child. He'd taken one of Adrian's toys with him, and he put it in the cot, in the crook of the baby's arm, and sat there watching mesmerised, half ecstatic, half terrified.

'I think I lost my mind,' he said. It was as if he had split into two people, the dull man who went to work every day and the freak who broke into people's houses to watch their children sleep.

He looked at me bleakly.

'What crimes have I committed?' he asked. 'Apart from trespass, adultery, cowardice, betrayal, selfishness, deceit and everything else?'

Before I could answer, he went on. 'I knew I didn't have the strength to confront Sylvia. I told myself that it was because I couldn't have been fully honest with her, about the years of longing, sitting in the attic with Adrian's things, breaking into other people's houses to watch their sleeping children, it was too much. But in fact I was too much a coward even to say the simplest thing, to tell her I'd fathered a child. And so,' he said, 'though I find it hard to believe now, I concocted the entire rigmarole to avoid having to do so.'

We sat for a while in silence. The washing machine was silent too. Bird noise came into the room from the street, a singing and a snapping.

At last, in answer to his question about crimes, I said that he had of course assumed a false identity, obtaining a bogus passport with which to exit the UK and enter Peru; and, furthermore, entered the US illegally; and, probably, broken American employment and financial laws regarding identity theft. Given that some of these events had happened many years earlier, that no other crimes had been committed more recently (so far as I knew), and that Adrian Palmer had subsequently lived as a law-abiding citizen in New York City, contributing to the economy and paying his federal taxes, it was possible the authorities in the UK and the US might not push for custodial sentences, though I couldn't be sure about that. In any case, my responsibility was simply to confirm his existence. I told him that I would file a report to which his wife would have access.

He considered all this. He knew, as I did, that there are various sorts of wrongdoing. I thought of Sylvia Bayliss as

194

I had last seen her, weeping on her enormous sofa. Perhaps he thought of her too.

He nodded at last. 'I'll take my chances,' he said.

Sarah joined him as he saw me out. They stood together at the top of their stoop, their arms round each other's waists. Don waved, the gesture of a kindly man, and I turned away and went down the street, under the trees, with the noises of children from the nearby playground, shrill and natural as birds.

Back in Bournemouth it was another lovely spring day. After I'd packed, I had an hour to wait before my taxi arrived to take me to the station, so I left the Ventry Arms and walked up the avenue for a last visit to Stevenson's memorial garden. It seemed nothing but an empty space to me now. Once a substantial house had filled it, stables, a kitchen garden. Sitting on a bench gazing at the partial traces of foundations in the turf and the meagre flower-beds surrounding them, I could imagine none of it. Other people's pasts disappear. What remains is the present. For Don Bayliss, though, the past had returned, and he didn't yet know how it would change his present. Nor did Louise, whose pleasure in bringing about the successful outcome was tempered by her uncertainty of what it might mean for her future workload and her apprehension at informing Sylvia Bayliss.

Sitting there in Stevenson's garden, I thought about the end of *Jekyll and Hyde*, the inevitable truth-telling, the final explanation, which seems, in fact, flat and only mildly interesting, for we had guessed the truth long before. We had already enjoyed the horrible shock of the revelation, and what is left, described in the explanatory letters of Doctors Lanyon and Jekyll, are the incidental details, the logistics of the plot. In a sense, the whole story has been about a missing person. First, it's Hyde who has gone missing. At the end, with Hyde dead on the floor of the dissecting room, it's Jekyll who is missing, who, indeed will never be found, for he no longer exists. But then neither Jekyll nor Hyde have ever truly existed as a separate man, for 'man is not truly one, but truly two', Stevenson says, and in fact not just two but many and multivarious.

Back at the Ventry Arms, I waited with my suitcase at a table set up on the lawn in front of the inn, until the taxi arrived. As I was about to get into it, one of the staff ran out to me with a package. Another guest had left it for me, she said.

It was a copy of John Fowles's *The Magus*. Mac had written inside *To help you keep looking* and there was a note with it telling me she was returning to Auckland, but 'not necessarily to Bag End'. I put it in my suitcase and got into the taxi, and gazed out of the window as we drove away down the pretty avenues.

ACKNOWLEDGEMENTS

For help given, sometimes inadvertently, it's my pleasure to acknowledge the following people: my agent, Anthony Goff, publisher Jon Riley, editor Jasmine Palmer, copy-editor Nick de Somogyi, PR directors Elizabeth Masters and Ana McLaughlin, and the wider team at Quercus, and – above all – my wife and children. Even if you didn't mean it, my thanks to you all.